"Making Love Didn't Change Anything, Blair."

Her eyes widened. "It changed *everything*."

"Not everything...but let me tell you what it did change." Ace tapped her chest with his forefinger. "Because you loved what we did, something in here will never be the same. You'll think of me whenever your blood heats up. You'll compare your fiancé's kisses to mine. And how he moves, what his attitudes are..."

"How could I compare attitudes? I don't know how *you* feel about anything!"

"I'd be glad to rectify that anytime you say the word," Ace said bluntly. "Stay the night with me. By morning you'll know everything there is to know about me."

Dear Reader,

When *Man of the Month* began back in 1989, no one knew it would become the reader favorite it is today. Sure, we thought we were on to a good thing. After all, one of the reasons we read romance is for the great heroes! But the program was a *phenomenal* success, and now, over six years later, we are celebrating our 75th *Man of the Month*—and that's something to be proud of.

The very first *Man of the Month* was *Reluctant Father* by Diana Palmer. So who better to write the 75th *Man of the Month* than this wonderful author? In addition, this terrific story, *That Burke Man,* is also part of her LONG, TALL TEXANS series—so it's doubly special.

There are also five more great Desire books this month: *Accidental Bride* by Jackie Merritt; *One Stubborn Cowboy* by Barbara McMahon; *The Pauper and the Pregnant Princess* by Nancy Martin—which begins her OPPOSITES ATTRACT series; *Bedazzled* by Rita Rainville; and *Texas Heat* by Barbara McCauley— which begins her HEARTS OF STONE series.

This March, Desire is certainly the place to be. Enjoy!

Lucia Macro,
Senior Editor

Please address questions and book requests to:
Silhouette Reader Service
U.S.: 3010 Walden Ave., P.O. Box 1325, Buffalo, NY 14269
Canadian: P.O. Box 609, Fort Erie, Ont. L2A 5X3

JACKIE MERRITT
ACCIDENTAL BRIDE

SILHOUETTE *Desire*

Published by Silhouette Books

America's Publisher of Contemporary Romance

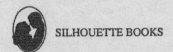

SILHOUETTE BOOKS

ISBN 0-373-05914-0

ACCIDENTAL BRIDE

Copyright © 1995 by Carolyn Joyner

This edition published by arrangement with Harlequin Enterprises B.V.

® and TM are trademarks of Harlequin Enterprises B.V., used under license. Trademarks indicated with ® are registered in the United States Patent and Trademark Office, the Canadian Trade Marks Office and in other countries.

Printed in U.S.A.

Books by Jackie Merritt

Silhouette Desire

Big Sky Country #466
Heartbreak Hotel #551
Babe in the Woods #566
Maggie's Man #587
Ramblin' Man #605
Maverick Heart #622
Sweet on Jessie #642
Mustang Valley #664
The Lady and the Lumberjack #683
Boss Lady #705
Shipwrecked! #721
Black Creek Ranch #740
A Man Like Michael #757
Tennessee Waltz #774
Montana Sky #790
Imitation Love #813
+*Wrangler's Lady* #841
+*Mystery Lady* #849
+*Persistent Lady* #854
Nevada Drifter #866
Accidental Bride #914

+Saxon Brothers series

Silhouette Books

Silhouette Summer Sizzlers
1994
"Stranded"

Montana Mavericks
The Widow and the Rodeo
  Man #2
The Rancher Takes a Wife #5

JACKIE MERRITT

and her husband live just outside of Las Vegas, Nevada. An accountant for many years, Jackie has happily traded numbers for words. Next to family, books are her greatest joy. She started writing in 1987 and her efforts paid off in 1988 with the publication of her first novel. When she's not writing or enjoying a good book, Jackie dabbles in watercolor painting and has been known to tickle the ivories in her spare time.

Prologue

It was all in fun. Blair Conover ducked into the fortune-teller's gaudy tent, laughing because Derek had been so insistent that she have her future told. The merry sounds of the carnival followed Blair inside, until the tent's flap dropped into place. Here, Blair noted, the music of the carousel was strangely muted.

"Please . . . sit down."

Blair jumped. The voice was female but deep and throaty, coming from a dark shadow.

"Uh . . . yes. Thank you." There was a small circular table with a deep red cloth and two chairs. Blair slid onto the one nearest the exit.

A woman stepped from the shadow. A dark blue scarf covered her hair. Her eyes were heavily made up, and she wore an inordinate amount of gold jewelry.

Or, rather, Blair thought wryly, Madam Morova was wearing a lot of *fake* gold jewelry. If all of those chains were real, the woman would be wearing a fortune around her neck, which wasn't likely in a traveling carnival.

Madam Morova took the opposite chair and placed her hands, palms up, on the table. She smiled. "You are young and very pretty. Please place your hands in mine."

Smiling tentatively, Blair complied. The woman's hands were warm and smooth. Madam Morova closed her eyes. Frowning slightly, recognizing just a touch of nervousness in herself, Blair gnawed on her bottom lip.

"I see an important event in your future. A wedding."

Blair smiled again, this time rather smugly. Her engagement ring had to be perfectly obvious to the woman.

"I see leaves . . . red and gold leaves. An autumn wedding."

"No," Blair rebutted. "My wedding is planned for—"

"Please, say nothing," the woman admonished. Blair closed her mouth. "An autumn wedding and...yes, a dark and handsome groom. He...is..." Madam Morova opened her eyes. "He is a stranger, but you will meet him very soon."

Well, thought Blair. This had to be the silliest waste of time and money she'd ever agreed to spend. The "groom" was *blond* and handsome, and waiting right outside the tent. Their wedding was going to be next month on a hot and sunny August day. And if Derek Kingston was a stranger, so was her brother, Mitch.

"Thank you," she said coolly, and withdrawing her hands from the woman's, started to rise.

"You do not believe what I told you because of another man in your life," Madam Morova said softly. "One who is familiar and comfortable."

Blair sank back to the chair seat.

"You are startled. Forgive me. I do not mean to frighten or alarm."

"What I am is engaged, Madam Morova. My fiancé is waiting outside for me at this very minute, and no stranger is going to suddenly appear and destroy our plans." Blair got to her feet. "Thank you for your time."

She swept from the tent and said, rather sharply, to Derek. "She's a fake, just like her cheap jewelry."

"Hon, I'm sorry. What did she tell you?" Derek took Blair's arm and they began walking through the crowd.

"She told me... Oh, it's too ridiculous to repeat." Blair smiled. "Weren't you going to treat me to some cotton candy?"

One

One

———

Blair maneuvered her car through traffic on Houghton's main business street, aptly named "Main Street," which normally wasn't a problem. But there was a political rally going on this Saturday. An incumbent state senator was in town, campaigning for reelection, and Houghton, Montana, was full of strangers.

The town had barely five thousand residents, although Blair figured the population was probably doubled today from all of the hoopla. Certainly many of the area's ranchers and farmers had come for the speeches and free food in the town park.

Blair wasn't interested in either free food or political speeches from this particular candidate. She had already decided that his opponent, a lady with a reputation for commonsense viewpoints and getting things done, would receive Blair Conover's vote.

Besides, Blair was concentrating on her shopping list, although Houghton had little to offer in the way of ingredients for the perfect wedding. Another trip to Billings was becoming more crucial with each stop she made, but she still had hopes of finding a few of the items on her list.

Blair worked for Houghton's largest bank. As a loan officer she had a responsible and satisfying job, and her salary wasn't half bad, either. Newcomers to the area were amazed at the business Houghton Security Bank conducted, but there were ranches—both large and small—in every direction from town, which kept Houghton's economy flowing.

Main Street had three traffic lights. At the first light, which was red, Blair braked and then ducked her head to see through the passenger window. The town's best dress shop, Redfern's, had changed its window display, and there was a striking black-and-white dress on a mannequin that definitely rated a second glance.

An impatient horn behind her brought Blair's gaze to the traffic light, which had turned green. She waggled her fingers up high, so the disgruntled driver behind her would see through her back window that she was sorry for gawking at Redfern's.

The next light was green, and Blair drove on through the intersection. Watching for a parking space in that block, unsuccessfully, Blair didn't notice the third light turning red until the last second.

She slammed on the brakes. A horrible crunching noise and a jolt from behind, strong enough to jar her teeth, came next. "Yipes!" she cried, and clutched the steering wheel in a death grip. Dazed but uninjured, thanks to her seat belt, Blair sat there.

Someone yanked her door open. "Are you all right?"

"I . . . guess so. Who ran into me?"

"I did. Are you sure you're all right?"

"Yes, I said! Why did you run into me?"

The man stood up with a disgusted grimace. "Oh, I was just driving along and thought to myself, now what can I do to make this a perfect day? I know, I'll run into that airhead up ahead in the blue Ford.''

"Airhead! Why, you..." Struggling with her seat belt, Blair finally got it unlatched. She stumbled out of the car. "If I'm an airhead, what does that make you? You ran into me, not the other way around! And for your information, tailgating is illegal! You're going to get a ticket, mister, and you're also going to pay for the damage to my car.''

Fuming, Blair stormed to the back of her car. She wailed out loud when she saw the broken taillights and crumpled trunk door. A crowd was gathering, and there were some familiar faces. "Joe, did you see this guy run into me?" she called.

Joe Whitley grinned. "Can't say I did, Blair. But I heard the crash.''

"Did anyone see me stop for the red light and this idiot plow into me?" she yelled.

"Calm down, will you?"

Blair whirled to face the culprit. "Don't tell me to calm down! You've practically totaled my car, you...you maniac!''

Thorpe Barclay—or Ace, as he preferred to be known—couldn't help laughing. Whoever this bubblehead was, she was pretty. Her long, kinky-curly hair was a dozen shades of sun-streaked blond, all natural, too, he'd bet. She had a lot of perfect white teeth, which flashed when she spoke. Or rather, when she yelled. Her green eyes contained more life than any eyes he'd ever seen, and all of that broiling energy was directed at him.

It was kind of exciting. *She* was exciting.

"I'll pay to have your car fixed," he told her.

"Where's a cop?" Blair yelled. "Has anyone seen anything of Brock Williams or Sonny Kelso?"

Joe Whitley piped up. "Brock and Sonny are at the park, Blair."

"Oh, great." Hands on hips, she faced her assailant again. "We're not moving these cars until Brock or Sonny sees what you did, understand?"

Traffic was piling up. Ace looked around and drawled, "Couldn't pick a better day for an accident, sugar."

"You should have thought of that before you day-dreamed your vehicle into mine, mister. And don't call me 'sugar'!"

"*I* daydreamed? Lady, did you once look at the road during the last four blocks? You were gawking at the stores, or the people, or at something. What's the matter? Don't you get to town very often?"

"I *live* in town, if it's any of your business! What's your name? And the name of your insurance company?"

"Ace Barclay's the name, and I happen to be flat out of car insurance."

Blair gave Barclay a scathing once-over. Ace? *Ace?* What a ridiculous name! He was long and lanky, bordering on thin. His jeans were worn and so were his boots. He had a head of unruly black hair, which certainly could use a trim, and the bluest eyes she had ever seen. It was startling to re-alize that she was staring at maybe the best-looking guy she'd ever come face-to-face with.

"Now, why doesn't that surprise me?" she said with as much sarcasm as she could manage, given the sudden odd awareness in her system.

"What's your name?"

"You ran into Blair Conover," she said coldly.

Ace grinned. "Should I be impressed?"

Realizing how patronizing she had just sounded, Blair had the grace to flush. But she was so damned mad. If she hadn't been wearing her seat belt, she might have been thrown all over the car.

"Look, I was only going about fifteen miles an hour," Ace said. "I didn't expect you to stop so suddenly."

"The light turned red, which any fool could see."

"I'm not a fool, Blair Conover."

The prideful way he said it made Blair give him a second look. Some of the spectators were wandering away, obviously becoming bored with the tableau. Traffic was getting past the accident, albeit at a snail's pace.

Blair was suddenly embarrassed for having yelled and thrown a tantrum on Main Street. "Well . . . I guess Brock and Sonny are busy at the park," she said in a quieter tone. "Give me your address and telephone number."

"I'll write it all down if you've got a piece of paper, sugar."

Fuming again because of that "sugar" business, Blair went into her car for her purse and found her notepad, from which she tore out a page, and a pen. "Here," she said while handing the items to Ace.

"Thanks." Ace placed the paper on top of her car and wrote his name, address and telephone number. He held the paper and pen out with a sassy grin. "Well, if I had to run into someone, I'm glad it was a pretty girl."

Blair stiffened. "Believe me, flattery is not going to make one dram of difference, Mr. Barclay. As soon as I get an estimate of damage, I'll be calling."

"I can hardly wait."

Blair delivered one more dirty look before shoving herself behind the wheel of her car. She hoped Ace Barclay understood how furious she was about this completely unnecessary accident. Now her car would have to be in the garage for God knew how long, and she had a million things to do before her wedding in three weeks.

Her car started just fine, and Blair drove off, making an immediate right turn to get away from Main Street. Any more shopping today was out. She had never been involved in a car accident before, and along with the anger careening around in her system, she felt a trifle unsteady.

Besides, the afternoon was passing. Derek was coming for supper, and a long soak before cooking seemed utterly crucial.

Blair was pulling into her driveway when a startling thought occurred to her: she had just met a dark, handsome stranger!

Turning off the ignition, she sat there and frowned, reminding herself that Madam Morova was a carnival fortune-teller, for Pete's sake. Coincidences happened every day. For that matter, Blair met new people through the bank all the time. Fate had not directed Ace Barclay—his awful name actually gave her a shiver—to ram his battered old pickup into the rear end of her much newer car.

Still, in retrospect, the incident didn't feel like just another left-handed introduction.

But acknowledging that bizarre fact annoyed Blair, and she got out of the car and went into her house wearing a grim expression. Hot baths had always been relaxing for Blair, and she could think of nothing she needed more at the moment.

The facts of her life, past and present, flitted through Blair's mind while she soaked in the large, old-fashioned tub in her house's one bathroom.

She had moved into this same house when she was eight. Her brother, Mitch, had been eleven, and both children had recently been shattered by the accidental death of their father. Attempting to pick up the pieces, their mother, Cheryl, bought the modest home with the little insurance money she received, and then went to work in a neighborhood grocery store to supplement a very modest monthly social security check to feed and clothe her fatherless children.

Mitch and Blair grew up fast. With very little extra cash in the family, they both displayed the ambition to find jobs and earn for themselves the things their mother couldn't afford to buy. Blair could barely remember a time when she didn't hold some kind of job. In junior high it had been baby-sitting. During high school there'd been miscellaneous jobs in the local stores, stock girl, some clerking, and then Blair's first real brush with business when a dry cleaner had her entering sales invoices into a ledger. Almost at once her ambition became focused on further education. Security was enormously important to her, and the business world beckoned.

During her youth, Derek Kingston had been initially in the foreground of Blair's existence and then somewhat less visible. For a time he and Mitch hung out together. But then Mitch's interest had swung to auto mechanics, while Derek's had landed on academics. Blair respected her brother's chosen vocation but personally found Derek's much more satisfying. She herself had no desire to teach school as Derek did, but educators, in her experience, were admired and looked up to.

It was after Derek graduated college, when he returned to teach fifth grade in Houghton, that he began coming around again. Mitch was working for a large paving contractor who was based in Seattle and temporarily in the area for some highway construction. Blair was still busy with her own education, commuting on a daily basis to Billings to attend classes in business administration.

For the first time Blair saw Derek's blond hair and even features as attractive. He was an old friend and welcome in the Conover home, in any case, but it thrilled her when she realized that he was coming to see her instead of Mitch.

They fell into an easy camaraderie. Derek was good company and nice-looking to boot. Blair was proud to be seen with him, and she definitely liked his low-pressure approach to romance. He understood her near obsession to making something of herself, and never once tried to talk her into a premature marriage and quitting school.

In the meantime, Cheryl began ailing. As her illness became serious, Blair and Derek grew closer. He was always there when she needed a shoulder to cry on, or a compassionate ear to listen to her worries about her mother.

The worst happened. Cheryl Conover passed away in a Billings hospital. Mitch was devastated, as was Blair, but she was also relieved that her beloved mother was beyond further suffering. Within weeks Mitch announced a permanent job offer from the Seattle paving contractor and moved to the West Coast. Blair finished her classes and obtained a job at the Houghton Security Bank.

For three years things ran pretty smoothly. Blair advanced at the bank until, now, at twenty-four years of age, she held a responsible position with what she considered to be a highly respected organization, strongly believing that her job was as secure as the bank itself.

Derek and Blair finally set their wedding date for the second Sunday in August. Blair knew that few people, if anyone, in Houghton would believe that she and Derek hadn't been sleeping together, but it was the God's truth. She wondered about her own high-mindedness, or whatever it was that kept her a virgin for so long, but she had no answers, other than the fact that she wasn't into risk taking. "Everything in good time" was a motto she kept to herself because it sounded overly prim, but she lived by it.

Derek, bless him, had gone along with her insistence on a very special wedding night. They planned a two-week honeymoon to Southern California, which Derek had visited and Blair had not. They would drive and sightsee along the way, and the trip was budgeted almost to the penny. One very positive thing about Derek, Blair ardently felt, was that she would never have to worry about him wasting their incomes.

Her future looked secure, which Blair liked. Madam Morova announcing everything going to hell because of a handsome stranger was too ludicrous to consider. She and Derek would continue to live in her house, which, of course, was equally owned by Mitch. But Mitch was building his own life in Seattle and had told her to not worry about his partial ownership. "Maybe someday you and Derek will want to buy me out, but there's no hurry on my part. I kind of like knowing I've still got roots in Houghton, Blair."

With her head against the back lip of the tub and her body getting pruny, Blair wished that Mitch were close enough to inspect her car. She would have to notify her own insurance company on Monday morning, of course, and it was intensely irritating that Barclay was that careless type of person who didn't carry insurance. She could probably cause him all sorts of trouble within the legal system, but maybe her insurance company would do that without her input.

At any rate, today's stupid accident was going to cost her time and trouble, even if Barclay paid every penny of the repair bill to put her car back in mint condition. She would accept no less, Blair decided vehemently, finally lifting herself from the soothing water and out of the tub.

After drying off she dressed in a skirt, blouse and sandals. With some makeup on her face, she finger-combed her tangle of curls and went to the kitchen to see to supper.

Derek arrived promptly—he always did—and greeted Blair with a warm but passionless kiss. She looked into his pleasant hazel eyes and thanked her lucky stars for her good fortune.

"A man ran his pickup into the back of my car on Main Street this afternoon."

Derek's smile faded. "You're all right?"

"I'm fine, but I can't say the same for my poor car."

"I'll go take a look."

Blair followed along to the garage, where Derek frowned at the damage. "You filed a police report, of course."

"Uh . . . Brock and Sonny were at the park. Traffic was snarled, and . . ."

Derek looked a bit displeased. "Do you know the guy?"

"No. But I have his address and telephone number."

"And the name of his insurance company?"

For some reason Blair felt guilty because Barclay didn't have insurance. It was just that Derek was so organized, and she couldn't imagine anyone without insurance having the gall to run into *his* car.

"Derek, his name is Ace Barclay, and he doesn't have insurance. He said he would pay for the damage, though, and I promised him, very distinctly, that indeed he would."

"I see. I wish I'd been there."

"To do what? What could you have done that I didn't?"

"Did you get the license number of Barclay's vehicle? Take a look at his driver's license?"

Blair felt herself blanching. "Uh . . . no."

"I know what happened, Blair. You got angry, didn't you?" Derek smiled indulgently. "Well, it's done and there's nothing we can do about it tonight. On Monday, though, you be sure and notify your insurance company first thing. They'll know what to do."

Feeling rather like a chastised child, Blair allowed Derek to lead her into the house, where he put his arms around her. She stood there stiffly and let him have his hug.

But then his hands slipped down her back to her hips, and she felt him drawing her closer. Quickly she moved out of reach. "I've got to check on supper."

It happened only once in a while, but every so often Blair felt Derek's desire. It never failed to unnerve her, because she believed they were single-minded on waiting for their wedding night, outdated attitude or not.

Still, it bothered her to keep saying no—she did love him, after all—and when Derek came into the kitchen, she said quietly, "It's only another three weeks, Derek."

"I know, Blair. Forget it. What're you fixing for supper?"

They sat outside after dinner in their favorite after-dark spot, the patio glider. Derek's arm was around Blair's shoulders and contentment permeated her soul, a feeling she had come to expect with her fiancé.

"So," she said softly. "What did you do today?"

"Sorted through those boxes of books I bought at the Hillman auction."

"That was nice," Blair murmured. Derek was an avid collector of old books, and while she didn't quite share his passion for out-of-print editions, she respected it.

"Get any shopping done today?" Derek inquired.

"Very little. I have to go to Billings next Saturday to finish up."

Derek squeezed her shoulder. "Won't be long now, will it, though there are times when three weeks seems like an eternity."

"No, it won't be long." Blair sighed.

"Something bothering you, Blair?"

"My car, of course. If I take it to the shop on Monday, do you think I'll have it back by the weekend?"

"It's possible. It might help to explain to Duane that you need it by the weekend."

"Derek, if it's not ready, could I use your car on Saturday?"

Derek cleared his throat. "Um...I guess I could drive you to Billings."

This wasn't the first time Blair had noticed Derek's reluctance to share his possessions, but this was most definitely the first time he'd done so with her. Of course, she'd never before had any reason to come right out and ask him for the use of something he prized.

She became quite still while debating the wisdom of pointing out what she considered to be a character flaw. She and Mitch had shared so much while growing up, and their mother had given all she could, whenever she could. Without that marvelous unselfishness, the Conover trio would have had a much harder time of it than they did.

Blair buried the impulse. Derek had so many wonderful qualities, and if he hesitated to turn his almost-new car over to another person, even her, she probably shouldn't judge him for it.

But in the back of her mind Blair vowed that she would either drive her own car to Billings next Saturday or ask a girlfriend to take her shopping.

Then, while they slowly rocked back and forth on the glider and Blair listened to the crickets chirping in the grass of the backyard, she thought of Ace Barclay. There was something untamed and exciting about the guy, and no woman honest enough to admit the truth could deny his good looks. His address was rural, so he must live on one of the ranches in the area. Probably worked as a cowhand.

One thing was certain: Ace Barclay was as different from Derek Kingston as day was from night. Oddly, Blair found herself concentrating on those differences and puzzling over the strange tingling in her body while she did it. When she realized what she was doing, she shook off the subject and, as though presenting an apology for even thinking about another man, she turned her face up for a kiss.

Derek gladly complied. His lips were warm and soft, and Blair thought about their wedding night. It was becoming clearer by the day that Derek was anxiously awaiting the big event, but was she? They'd known each other for so long and she loved him dearly. But why wasn't she impatient at the passage of time, as he was? Why didn't she tremble at his touch, as he did at hers?

His tongue sought entrance to her mouth, and Blair pulled back. To alleviate the impact of her silent rebuff, she smiled. "Are you still going to that auction near Miles City tomorrow?"

"Did you change your mind about coming along?"

Blair gave her head a shake. "I've got to talk to Katie McPherson about the cake, and go over to Millie's for a fitting." Millie Dodge was Houghton's only resident dressmaker, and Blair had gone to Millie for her wedding gown.

With school out for the summer, Derek had been working at two different part-time jobs. First, he was tutoring youngsters who needed special attention, and secondly, he put in several days each week at Hannigan's shoe store. He kept his weekends free to coincide with Blair's work schedule, but she had been so busy with wedding plans for the past month, their "dates" had been pretty much confined to quiet evenings together.

"I should be back in time for dinner tomorrow," Derek said. "Shall we eat out?"

He hated eating out, Blair knew, having heard him state many times that restaurant food was not worth the cost. Which was probably the truth in Houghton, as its restaurants and cafés were nothing to get excited about. But as practical as Blair was about money, sometimes the thought of cooking was downright nauseating.

Again she buried words that were right on the tip of her tongue. "I'll throw something together," she offered, and sensed Derek's relief.

"Well, guess I'd better be going," he said. "It's getting late."

It couldn't be much after ten, but Blair, too, was ready to call it a day. "I'll walk you to your car."

They left the patio and made their way around the side of the house to the driveway. Derek locked his hands together behind Blair's waist and pulled her forward for a good-night kiss.

She closed her eyes and realized something rather shattering: she could kiss Derek and feel next to nothing. When he raised his head, she searched his face in the dim light. How could that be? How could she be in love with Derek and feel so little when he kissed her? When she kissed him?

That would change, wouldn't it? After they made love? Once she experienced the full scope of adult passion?

With Derek's car disappearing down the dark street, Blair slowly returned to the back of the house and the patio. Instead of going in, she sat on the glider. Why was she so questioning tonight? So unsettled?

A sudden image in her mind of dark, unruly hair and sassy blue eyes startled her, and she leapt up from the glider and ran inside. Snapping off lights as she tore through the house, she stopped in her dark bedroom to catch her breath.

Instantly her thoughts became very determined. She was in love with Derek and they were going to be married in three weeks. And no overly macho guy was going to interfere, by damn, especially not a careless, reckless individual like Ace Barclay!

Two

Blair looked out the front window of her house the next morning to see two men coming up her sidewalk. One of them was more than a little overweight and wearing a huge cowboy hat. The other was Ace Barclay.

She was dressed, thank goodness, but if Barclay had arrived fifteen minutes sooner, she would have been answering the door in her bathrobe.

Or maybe she wouldn't have answered it at all. Maybe she *shouldn't* answer it now! What was he doing here?

Blair let the man knock twice before opening the door with a deliberately cool, "Yes?"

"Hi." Ace presented a big friendly grin. Blair Conover looked like a sweet treat this morning in her pale green shorts and sleeveless blouse, maybe, given the frosty expression in her green eyes, like creamy mint sherbet. "Remember me?"

Blair rolled her eyes. "How could I forget?"

"I need a favor."

Blair couldn't help smirking. "*You* came to *me* for a favor?" She glanced to the other man, who was grinning all over his cherubic face. "Do you need a favor, too?"

The man guffawed but had the grace to blush, Blair saw. "No, ma'am. I'm only here because of Ace."

Blair returned her gaze to Barclay, and she absolutely, positively refused to acknowledge his chiseled good looks. "Why are you here?" she questioned bluntly.

"I'd like ol' Virge here to take a look at your car."

"Why?"

"'Cause he's a first-rate body-and-fender man, and I'd like to hear his opinion."

"Oh? Do you work for Duane Kemp, Mr.... uh, Virge? As far as I've been aware, Duane has the only body-and-fender shop in the area."

"Heck, no," Virge replied with a snicker. "I work for Ace."

"For Ace," Blair repeated, and turned a scathing gaze back to the younger, taller man. "No one but a professional is going to touch my car, Mr. Barclay."

"I knew you'd feel that way, which is why I brought ol' Virge along," Ace replied smoothly. "It wouldn't hurt anything for him to have a look, would it?"

"That's possibly a debatable point." Blair held the door and thought for a moment. Ace Barclay wore a totally innocent expression, slightly expectant, and "ol' Virge" just stood there looking rather silly.

These two could be a deadly duo. Any devilry one couldn't think up, the other probably did. Ol' Virge was no more than a few years older than his pal, Ace, whom Blair estimated to be around thirty, and she didn't trust either of them as far as she could throw them.

But maybe they had their own logical reason for wanting to examine her car. She finally sighed. "All right. I'll open the garage door from the inside." With that, she firmly closed the door in Ace Barclay's face.

The two men wandered from the front of the house to the driveway. "Hell, Ace," Virgil Potter said matter-of-factly. "She's even prettier than you said. But she sure don't like you none."

"Is that how you see it?" Ace declared with mock incredulity. He grinned. "Bet I can make her like me a whole lot."

"Bet you can't."

"How much?"

"Uh . . . twenty bucks."

"It's a bet."

Virge shifted his considerable weight. "How will we know who won?"

Ace's grin never wavered. "How about when I take her out the first time, I let you know where we're going and you just happen to run into us?"

Virge nodded. "That'd do it."

The garage door began creaking upward. Blair ducked beneath it before it came to a shuddering halt. "Go ahead and take your look, Mr. Barclay, but don't be long. I'll be using the car in about ten minutes." She turned to go.

"Don't run away, sugar," Ace drawled.

Blair stopped abruptly and turned slowly. "I'm not running, Mr. Barclay, and neither do I answer to 'sugar.'" The man's maddening grin clearly stated that she'd just done exactly that, and Blair felt a flush creeping into her cheeks.

"Is 'Ace' too tough to remember, honey? No one calls me *mister*."

Blair wondered what there was about Ace Barclay that rubbed her so wrong, outside of his insolent grin and chauvinistically superior attitude, that is. Obviously he was full of himself, peacock-proud of his lean, lithe body and startlingly handsome features.

But she had a vague sense of something tightly coiled and sensually dangerous beneath his laid-back drawl and flirty expressions, and that was what she couldn't quite comprehend or deal with. For a moment memory taunted.

"Mom, how did you meet Dad? And how did you know you loved him?"

Cheryl Conover laughed. *"The first time I set eyes on your dad I got weak in the knees. The second time was at a church social and my stomach hurt so much I couldn't eat a bite. Oh, it was love, Blair, make no mistake, the kind of love that knocks the stuffing out of a gal."*

But having the "stuffing knocked out of her" didn't appeal to Blair. Ace Barclay's sassy blue eyes did strange things to her nervous system, and neither did she find quivering nerves appealing.

It helped to concentrate on Derek while looking at Ace, she realized, which she did to the point of relaxing some. "There's no earthly reason for you and I to be on a first-name basis, Mr. Barclay."

With that, Blair left the man standing in the driveway while his friend Virge inspected the damage to her car. She went around the house to the backyard and then stopped to wonder why she couldn't immediately remember what she had intended doing next.

Oh, yes, she'd been getting ready to drive over to Katie McPherson's house to discuss the decorations for the wedding cake. Blair started for the patio slider to go inside.

"Nice place you got here."

Blair whirled. "Mr. Barclay! My backyard is not public domain. I thought you wanted to inspect my car."

"I wanted ol' Virge to inspect your car," Ace reminded in an unconcerned voice while he looked around. "You've got terrific landscaping back here. Did you plant all these perennials?"

"My mother did."

"Oh, you live with your mother."

"My mother is dead, Mr. Barclay. I live alone."

"Sorry you lost your mother, Blair, but I can't find it in me to be sorry you live here all by your lonesome." Ace's outlaw grin appeared at full throttle. "I'd sure like the chance to get to know you better, honey."

A wave of warmth colored Blair's neck and face. "I'm engaged to be married, Mr. Barclay. In three weeks." An enormous satisfaction developed within Blair at the startled expression on Ace's face.

But then his grin returned. "Doesn't give me much time, does it?"

"To do what?" Blair inquired caustically.

"What do you think?"

Blair's color deepened again. "I *think* you're crude and . . . and rude!"

Virge's voice interrupted. "Hey, Ace!"

"I'm in the backyard."

Virge came around the house. "Wha'cha doing back here?"

Ace's eyes remained on Blair. "Just talking." He looked at his friend. "What do you think about this pretty lady's car?"

"It needs work, all right. About eight, nine hundred bucks' worth, I'd estimate."

Ace sighed. "Figured that. Virge, why don't you wait in the pickup while I talk to this sweet-tempered lady?"

"Sure, Ace."

Uh, oh, thought Blair, suspecting some kind of scam in the making. Virge was barely out of sight when she said, coldly, "Don't suggest anything but normal procedure for repairing my car, Ace."

"You said my name and it didn't hurt a bit, did it?"

"And don't waste my time with silly talk. I'm not one bit interested in you beyond your checkbook!"

"An honest woman, as I live and breathe," Ace said with a teasing laugh. "But, sugar, the balance in my checking account right now wouldn't buy a cup of coffee."

"You can't pay for the repairs, can you?" Blair shrieked.

"Not today I can't. I'd like to cut a deal with you."

"No deals! I'm going to turn this whole fiasco over to my insurance company in the morning, and I hope they sign a complaint for your arrest!"

"If they send me to jail, would you bake me a cake with a file in it, sugar?"

"Don't make fun of me, Ace. You're a menace on the streets, and I wouldn't doubt if you're a menace to women in general."

Ace laughed. "Scare you, don't I? I wonder why. Ask yourself why an engaged-to-be-married woman is all shivery because another man thinks she's just about the sexiest, prettiest little thing he's ever seen."

"I am not all shivery," Blair rebutted hotly. "You're revolting." She started for the slider again. "I'm going in. Please don't come back here again."

"Blair?"

The way he said her name sent a rippling thrill up Blair's spine, which infuriated her. She turned with angrily flashing eyes. "What now?"

"Are you really going to insist on regular procedure when I could get your car fixed without it costing me money I don't have right now?"

For the first time he sounded like a normal person with maybe one too many problems. Blair's innate compassion kicked in. "Uh...my own insurance company will pay the bill if you can't."

"Not without coming after me first, they won't. Insurance companies don't pay out money they don't have to, honey."

Blair had always been influenced by commonsense arguments, and who knew better than she how disturbing it was for a person to have financial worries? Her mother, Mitch and herself had lived with that weighty burden for a good many years.

Relenting wasn't easy, however. Derek wouldn't like it if she deviated from the straight-and-narrow path with the car repairs, and she, herself, preferred doing things by the book.

She took in Ace's clean but unquestionably shopworn clothing. His ancient jeans were maybe a tad too snug and bore a few holes. His shirt was plain and a survivor of countless washings. Ace had rolled up the sleeves, which somehow looked sexier on him than rolled-up sleeves did on Derek.

But it was the plea in his blue, blue eyes that was Blair's final undoing. Her own brother had used that very expression on her when he was in bad need of help with a problem, and it had never failed to influence her.

"You're an unscrupulous man," she mumbled. "But what's your deal?"

"I knew you had a tender heart the second I saw you, Blair, honey."

"Maybe stupid is more appropriate than tender. Tell me your deal."

"Well, it's this. Let me take your car out to my place where Virge can work on it. He's got the right tools out there, and..."

"Your place! I don't even know where you live!"

"You've got my address. Better yet, drive out yourself. I'd be happy to bring you back to town."

This whole thing was getting unnerving, but Blair didn't know how to refuse point-blank when Ace Barclay obviously didn't have two cents to his name. What *would* her insurance company do? Despite hurling wishes about Ace being arrested, she really didn't want the law on his back because of her.

But neither could she hand over the keys to her car to a stranger. A *peculiar* stranger.

"Let me...think about it," she said weakly. "Why don't I call you sometime tomorrow? Will you be at the number you gave me?"

"Sure will."

Blair twirled a curl at her ear, which Ace found utterly fascinating. "Uh...just for my information, would Virge have it fixed by next weekend? I need to go to Billings on Saturday?"

"Don't see why not," Ace said absently, still staring at that tawny curl being wound around her forefinger.

"And you're positive he knows what to do?"

"No question about it. Ol' Virge worked in a body-and-fender shop for two years a while back. He's a pro."

Derek will hate this. Worriedly Blair scrunched her forehead into a half-dozen tiny lines.

From out of nowhere a knot began developing in Ace's stomach. The pressure he'd been putting on Blair Conover was necessary. He was as close to being broke as he'd ever been. But suddenly he wanted to explain to Blair *why* he was broke, and *why* his insurance policy had lapsed.

She wasn't just pretty, she was the softest-looking, sexiest bundle he'd ever been near. Her big green eyes were making something in his chest do a weird flip-flop, and there wasn't any doubt in his mind that another area of his anatomy was misbehaving because she was almost close enough to touch.

Hey, Barclay, he thought. This isn't like you. Slow down, man.

The *sugar*s and *honey*s he'd been tossing around echoed as shallow and empty in his own brain. Blair Conover didn't deserve the big come-on treatment, not when she looked ready to cry because of his manipulation.

Every drop of cockiness disappeared from his expression. "I've got a better idea, Blair. Call your insurance company in the morning, as you planned. You have to report the accident or risk losing your coverage. Tell them the guy who ran into you promised to fix your car, but if he doesn't, you'll be contacting them again. Then give me a call, and I'll either pick up the car or you can drive it out to my place tomorrow evening."

Blair became very still, even the finger in her hair. Before her very eyes Ace Barclay had, without warning, turned into a nice guy, and the change in him seemed to arrow right to the core of her.

Never had she seen bluer eyes or a more kissable mouth on a man. She licked her lips, not quite wondering what a kiss from him would feel like, but getting very close to the unseemly and uncharacteristic conjecture.

He's a gunslinger, she thought with a sinking sensation. The old term, used in high school by Blair and her girl-friends when giggling about a boy on the make, flashed into her mind and remained. She hadn't thought of it in years, but then, it had been that long since she'd been near a guy who fit the word so accurately.

What was so hard to digest was how a man like Ace—a gunslinger—made a woman feel. She wasn't thinking of high-school boys and girls now, she was thinking of men and women, and how incredibly different two men could be from each other. Derek could look at her with love in his eyes and not make her legs go rubbery, while Ace could look at her with nothing more than sass and brass in his and she got all flustered and female.

Ace wasn't sure what was going on behind her green eyes, though he was picking up some very unexpected vibes. "Blair?"

"I..." Her breath deserted her.

Ace took a forward step, shaken by the electricity arcing between them. "Look... I've got some explaining to do, and..."

"No...please." Blair backed up and found herself against the slider door. "I'll call you tomorrow. Goodbye." Yanking the slider open, she darted into the house and quickly closed herself in. Her last glimpse of Ace, before she hastily left the glass door, was of him standing on her patio with a perplexed, slightly stunned expression.

But if Ace was stunned, Blair was knocked for a loop. Trembling, she went to the living room window and positioned herself to see out without giving her presence away. Ace slowly walked around the house, crossed her small front yard and climbed into his pickup truck.

Blair could see him and Virge talking, and wondered what they were discussing, her or her car.

The conversation *wasn't* about cars, dented or otherwise.

"The bet's off, Virge," Ace said gruffly.

"How come?"

Ace started the engine. "I don't wanna talk about it, okay?"

Virge grinned. "Maybe you already struck out."

"Just drop it," Ace growled.

"Well, heck, you don't need to get mad."

Derek came in around seven. He hugged Blair and kissed the cheek she turned up. "Sorry I'm so late."

Blair had been on edge ever since Ace's visit. "I didn't cook anything, Derek. I'd like to go out and do something fun."

"Fun? Like what?"

She saw the pained expression on his face and felt her need for "something fun" losing impetus. Turning away, she sighed. "Forget it. I have a package of that smoked turkey you like, and I'll make some sandwiches for dinner."

Derek brightened. "That would be great, hon. You're sure, though? If you really want to eat out ..."

"No, it's all right. Come to the kitchen and talk to me. Did you buy anything at the auction today?"

Derek perched on a counter stool. "Their books were a laugh, Blair. Mostly paperbacks with torn covers. It was a long drive for nothing."

"I'm sorry."

"Did you get the cake design worked out with Katie?"

"Yes, and I went for a fitting on my dress."

Derek smiled. "I'll bet it's beautiful."

"It is," Blair acknowledged quietly. The dress was a dream, actually. Millie Dodge had outdone herself on a difficult pattern with countless gores, bits of inset lace and seed pearls.

"You seem a little down tonight," Derek said then. "Anything wrong, hon?"

This was the moment to pass on Ace Barclay's plea, Blair knew. But she couldn't face the lecture Derek would most assuredly deliver because she had even listened to Ace's proposal, let alone considered it.

Blair wondered, unhappily, just when Derek had become a person to whom she couldn't talk freely. She had always thought of him as understanding, but on closer examination she realized that most of that understanding had been prior to setting their wedding date.

At any rate, she knew she wasn't going to mention Ace or his proposal tonight, which bothered her. Deliberately backing off from a controversial subject was no way to begin a lifelong commitment, which was precisely how Blair viewed marriage. And this weekend she had avoided controversy twice with Derek. How many other times had she done the same thing without realizing it?

"Blair? Are you all right?" Derek questioned.

"I'm fine. Just a little tired." Another lie. What she was was keyed up, internally restless.

"Well, I'll leave early, hon. Let you get to bed at a sensible hour."

Derek was true to his word. They ate to the accompaniment of a detailed accounting of Derek's afternoon at the estate auction, cleaned up the few dishes and said goodnight. At the last minute, just before Derek walked out the door, Blair suffered a horrible pang of guilt and threw her arms around her fiancé's neck.

He responded with a long kiss, during which Blair forced herself to concentrate on pleasure and affection.

It horrified her to see Ace Barclay's image behind her closed eyelids, and she pulled away abruptly. "Good night, Derek."

He was frowning. "You really are tired, aren't you? Blair, are you positive you weren't injured in that accident yesterday?"

His concern made Blair flinch from another barrage of guilt. "I'm positive." She improvised. "It's probably just the wedding plans, Derek. There are so many details to take care of."

"You're doing a terrific job, hon. Our wedding is going to be the talk of Houghton." Smiling indulgently, Derek gave her another kiss, this one brief and emotionless. "Get a good night's sleep. You'll be your usual bright self in the morning."

There were always chores to do on Sunday night. Blair's routine was to iron and press the clothing she would wear to the bank during the following week. She forced herself to set up the ironing board and plug in the iron, but her restlessness tonight precluded her usual enthusiasm for wardrobe planning.

When the task was finished, Blair breathed a sigh of relief and went to her room to get ready for bed. Once into her pajamas, however, she wandered the dark house rather than settling down for the night.

She didn't like the uneasiness in her system, where only a few days ago there'd been contentment. It was Ace Barclay's doing, but she couldn't lay all of the blame on him. Undoubtedly he treated her the same way he did all reasonably attractive women, and it wasn't his fault that an idiotic part of herself she hadn't even known existed had suddenly come alive.

Loving Derek was a given, but Blair knew that it was a love without excitement, without any of the giddiness and foolish palpitations she had endured under Ace's scrutiny today. How did a man do that to a woman with a mere look? How did a few minutes of exposure to sheer sex appeal cause such damage as she was feeling now?

Unnerving as it was, it had no meaning. She certainly would never trade her solid, secure future with a man of Derek's caliber for some excitement with an outlaw like Ace Barclay. In all honesty, she would prefer never seeing the man again.

But there was the car matter to consider. What in God's name was she going to do about her car? If Ace was plain and colorless she would help him out in a heartbeat. Obviously he was in a financial jam, and never would she forget how economically beaten her mother had been at times after losing her husband. But there was Derek's attitude to consider, and Blair knew she would have to confess what she was doing, should she go along with Ace's plan.

By the time Blair had worried the situation to shreds, she was tired enough to sleep.

Still, it was disheartening even in her torpid, semiconscious state just before oblivion to realize that her last lucid thoughts of the day were centered on a sassy, sexy mouth and a pair of electric blue eyes.

Three

——

Blair had no more than walked into Houghton Security's sedate brick building on Monday morning when the telephone on her desk began ringing. Although the bank's doors hadn't yet opened for business, she picked up the phone with her usual brisk, "Blair Conover. May I help you?"

"Hi, Blair. This is Winona. Listen, I called in sick today, so I won't be there. But I remembered an appointment for this morning and was wondering if you would take care of it for me."

Winona Schnieder was the bank's other loan officer, and the two women had a good working relationship. "Sure, Winona, glad to do it. What's wrong with you?"

"Just a bug. Came down with it yesterday. I'm feeling a little better today, but I haven't been able to get very far away from the house, if you know what I mean."

"I understand," Blair said sympathetically. "Where's the info on your appointment?"

"There's a folder in the top middle drawer of my desk. It's the only one, so you won't have any trouble identifying it. There's not much in it as the guy's coming in this morning to fill out a loan ap."

"I'll take care of it. Oh, what time?"

"Eleven."

After goodbyes, Blair put away her purse and went over to Winona's desk for the folder. Returning to her own desk, she set the folder aside, knowing through past experience that it contained only Winona's hand-scrawled notes. Mr. Whatever-his-name-was had apparently made a preliminary approach to negotiating a loan, probably dropping by the bank to inquire about current interest rates.

New loan customers were taken by Blair and Winona on an informal basis. Whichever one of them was free when a customer walked in talked to him or her. There were bank bonuses paid to the loan officers based on completed loans, so a good solid client was valued by both women.

But Winona and Blair hadn't let competition get in the way of friendship, and they often assisted with each other's customers.

As the bank's other employees began opening up for business, Blair frowned at the phone. After a minute, deciding to get the unsettling chore out of the way, she looked up her insurance agent's number and dialed it.

At five minutes to eleven, Ace strode into Houghton Security Bank and stopped to look around. The tellers were busy, phones were ringing, and customers were involved with various activities. He had seen the same productive business atmosphere during his initial visit to the bank last week.

When it became apparent that he would have to borrow money to keep going, Ace had made inquiries among the people he'd become acquainted with in the area: Houghton Security had been recommended more often than the town's other two banks, which had been good enough for him.

But the desk at which Winona Schneider had been sitting when he first talked to her was vacant today, which surprised him. His gaze went beyond Winona's desk to another, and he froze. Blair Conover worked here? Why hadn't he seen her last week?

She had to have been out that day, because he knew he never would have overlooked her. She wasn't a woman that any man would overlook. Today her untamed curls were subdued into a loosely structured braid at the back of her head, and the bright color of her hair seemed to glow in contrast to the dignified, gray-and-white outfit she was wearing. Her head was down while she concentrated on an array of papers on her desk. She looked cool, calm and collected, and Ace felt her where it counted, deep in the pit of his stomach.

He took a breath and told himself to cool it. Blair Conover was another man's property, or she would be in three weeks, and he didn't believe in poaching.

But he didn't object to a little innocent flirting, and Blair was a sweetheart. Shaping a cocky grin, he crossed the lobby and headed directly to Blair's desk. "'Morning, babe."

Startled, Blair brought her eyes up. "Ace! What are you doing here?"

"I've got an appointment with Winona Schneider. But I don't see her."

"*You're* Winona's eleven o'clock appointment?" Blair sighed. "Sit down. She's out today and asked me to see you."

Ace just stood there. Spilling his life story for any reason was bad enough, but doing so to Blair Conover's pretty face didn't sit well. "Maybe I should come back when Winona's here. Will she be in tomorrow?"

"She's home ill, so I really couldn't say." Blair waved at the two chairs in front of her desk. "Sit down, Ace. Winona and I work with each other's loan applicants all the time."

Which meant, he thought uneasily, Blair would have access to his file however he tried to keep her out of it. Not that he had anything to hide, but he never had been one to spread around his private affairs.

In the end, reluctantly bowing to inevitability, Ace took a seat.

"I didn't know you worked here," he told Blair while watching her stack the papers on her desk to clear a space for a file folder.

"That makes us even. I didn't know you were one of Winona's customers."

Blair reached into a drawer for an application form. "She said you wanted to apply for a loan. This is the form we'll use. You answer the questions, I fill it out," she explained.

"Great," Ace mumbled.

Blair regarded him across the desk. He looked only incredible today, wearing a blue shirt the same color as his eyes, and much newer jeans than she'd seen on him so far. His hair still needed a trim but was neatly brushed, and he just looked so crisp and handsome, she felt an absurd urge to stare.

She dropped her gaze to the application form and picked up a pen. "Last name, Barclay," she murmured while writing within the appropriate space. "First name..."

"Thorpe."

Blair looked up. "Thorpe," she repeated. "Apparently 'Ace' is a nickname."

"Apparently."

"Middle name?"

"Wilson."

Blair smiled to herself and repeated softly, "Thorpe Wilson Barclay."

Ace snorted derisively. "Don't know what my folks were thinking about when they saddled me with that moniker."

"It's a very nice name," Blair rebutted. "Date of birth?"

Ace recited his birth date, his address and then his social security number.

Blair cleared her throat. "Marital status?"

"I've never been married."

Checking the tiny box beside "Single," Blair also checked her strange surge of relief. She hadn't thought of him as married, he hadn't *seemed* married, but one didn't really know a person from two brief contacts.

"The rest is financial information," she said in her most professional voice. "We'll start with assets."

Ace took a long breath. "There aren't many. The ranch is fifteen hundred acres..."

"You own a ranch?"

"I bought the old Sutter place."

Blair sat back. "I know the place. Isn't it badly run-down?"

"Not as run-down as it was a few weeks back."

"You've been fixing it up?"

"It's the reason I'm in here for a loan. I underestimated the cost of repairs and ran out of money."

Toying with the pen in her hand, Blair took Ace's reluctant expression to mean he wasn't thrilled with so much candor.

But candor was absolutely necessary for a loan. "What do you owe on the place?" she questioned.

"Nothing."

"No mortgage of any kind?"

"Paid the Sutter family in cash. I thought I had enough money left to make the necessary repairs and get by until the fall cattle sale, but some unexpected problems cleaned me out."

"What kind of problems?"

"The worst was the existing well going dry. Had to locate a new water point and drill another well."

"A costly venture and a lot of red tape," Blair commented, aware of the county's strict regulations regarding water usage, particularly new pipelines into the area's aquifer.

"It busted me," Ace confirmed flatly.

It wasn't easy for Blair to alter her initial opinion of Ace Barclay. He still looked like an outlaw, like a gunslinger, sitting across her desk with all that black hair and macho confidence. She had never seen a better-looking man in her life, except for the movies, but watching a handsome actor toss sex appeal all over the screen was vastly different than dealing with the same qualities in person.

The bottom line was that Ace didn't look or even act like a solid citizen but, apparently, was exactly that. The bank's loan committee would, of course, consider his loan application, providing other factors checked out.

"We'll need three things to get started," Blair said quietly. "An appraisal of your property, a title search, and a report on your credit history. You will have to pay the costs of obtaining that information. Did Winona fill you in on points and interest rates?"

"Yeah, she did. About the costs of those reports, will I have to pay them up front?"

The bank's stringent but sensible rules looked crass to Blair in this instance. "I'm afraid so." At the sudden fierce pride she saw in Ace Barclay's eyes, she added quickly, "I don't need a check today, Ace. It will be up to Winona to order the reports. In the meantime, let me get your previous address."

Tight-lipped, Ace recited a Colorado address. Writing it on the form, Blair thought of other questions she would like to ask. How did you come by enough cash to buy the Sutter ranch? Why did you choose Montana? And—most disturbing—how are you going to survive if the loan committee turns down your loan application?

"Let's finish up with assets and liabilities," she said instead. "You mentioned cattle."

"Four hundred head of Red Angus. They came with the place. All healthy."

"Any other livestock?"

"Six horses. They came with me."

"Equipment?"

Ace listed various pieces of ranch equipment and then added with a short laugh, "My 1983 Chevy pickup, which you've seen for yourself."

"Uh...yes." After writing it down, Blair's eyes lifted. "I reported the accident to my insurance agent."

Ace cocked an eyebrow. "And?"

"He has no objections to your repairing my car, but he made one rather strong suggestion, that you sign a Consent of Liability form."

"What is it?"

"An acknowledgment of liability, I guess. Do you have any objections to signing it?"

Ace shook his head. "Nope, no objections. Do you have one of those forms?"

"He's having one dropped off here at the bank sometime today. I'll see that you get it."

Ace leaned forward slightly. "Then you're going to let Virge fix your car?"

Blair heaved a silent sigh. Until this moment she hadn't really made up her mind. "Yes. I'll bring it and the form by your place...tomorrow evening." This evening was going to be taken up with an explanation to Derek. She simply could not make a decision of this nature and deliberately leave Derek out of it.

Sitting back again, Ace soberly regarded the beautiful young woman across the desk. She reached him in an unfamiliar way. In a familiar way, as well, but he didn't need to examine his physical reactions to Blair Conover to understand them. But there was so much more to her than a pretty face, and it was disturbing to recognize within himself the sort of strong, compelling attraction to a woman that made a man sit up and take notice.

"Blair, I apologize for calling you an airhead the other day," he said quietly. "Obviously you're anything but." The apology surprised Ace as much as it did Blair, and they looked at each other intently throughout a long moment.

Blair broke the spell with a brief laugh. "I owe *you* an apology for gawking at everything but the light turning red." Although her heart seemed to be beating much faster than normal, she forced her attention back to the application form. "What debts do you owe, and to whom?"

"I don't owe anyone anything. Other than you."

"You have no debts at all?" It was rare when a loan applicant didn't have liabilities. Blair suspected that the committee wouldn't have much trouble approving Ace's request for a loan.

"None. Listen, I'd like to explain about my vehicle insurance."

"If you wish."

"I was lax about notifying everyone of my change of address," Ace confessed. "By the time a routine notice of premium due caught up with me, I was out of money. I called the insurance company and they said they would reinstate my policy when they received my check, but I couldn't send it."

In the back of Blair's mind was a worry about how he would come up with the approximately five hundred dollars needed to get the loan started, the cost of those crucial reports. But she would leave any discussion on that matter in Winona's capable hands.

The application was complete, other than Ace's signature. Blair read it over, ostensibly to make sure she had missed nothing. But once signed, Ace would be getting up from his chair and leaving, and envisioning herself returning to her own duties created a strange rebellion in her system.

He was, obviously, a much more complex individual than she had thought. Why the cocky *honey*s and *sugar*s when the side of him that she was seeing now was so pleasant?

Finally, unable to put it off any longer, Blair slid the form across the desk and held out a pen. "Check the information I entered for accuracy, then sign the line I've indicated with an *X*."

Ace scanned the form. "Looks fine to me." He scrawled his signature and laid down the pen. "Is that it?"

"Almost," Blair confirmed. She was writing on a small pad. Finished, she tore off the top sheet and handed it to him. "These are items the bank will need to process your application. You needn't bring in originals. Copies will do just fine."

Ace read aloud. "Federal tax returns for the past two years. Verification of any income for this year. Deed to the ranch. Bills of Sale on the livestock." He looked up. "Do I bring these things to you?"

"To Winona."

Folding the paper and slipping it into his shirt pocket, Ace asked casually, "So, what do you think? Have I got a shot at a loan?"

"I shouldn't be passing out that sort of opinion, but if everything you told me checks out, I would say you have a very good shot."

Ace got to his feet. "It'll check out." He placed his hands on Blair's desk and leaned over it. "Will what you told me about yourself check out?"

"Uh..." Nervously Blair glanced around. Customers didn't ordinarily lean over desks in Houghton Security. "What did I tell you?"

"That you're getting married in three weeks," Ace said softly.

Blair dampened her lips. "I am."

"Does your guy know how lucky he is?"

She shaped a weak smile. "Maybe I'm the lucky one."

Ace looked at her, capturing her gaze with his. "I doubt that. See you tomorrow night, okay?"

"Yes...tomorrow night."

"And you know how to find my place?"

"Yes."

Ace straightened his back and grinned. "So long, sugar."

Wide-eyed and startled, Blair watched his long-legged stride carry him through the lobby to the front door. Why had he done that? Why, after behaving like a normal and very likable person throughout the interview, had he reverted to cockiness and called her "sugar" again?

Suddenly depressed for no good reason that she could think of, Blair slipped Ace's application form into Winona's folder and slapped it closed. "Thorpe Wilson Barclay," she muttered. Now, why would a man with a wonderful name like that allow people to call him "Ace"?

Blair didn't think of herself as conniving or manipulative, but she prepared one of Derek's favorite dishes for dinner that evening, a chicken-and-vegetable stir-fry. For dessert, she served cherry cheesecake, another favorite, and steaming hot coffee.

Her efforts earned her loads of praise from Derek, which until recently would have warmed the cockles of her heart.

Tonight she merely smiled and said thank you until she got tired of doing so. Her mind was elsewhere, on the accident, on Ace Barclay, on her upcoming wedding, on the future, the past and the disturbing present. She told herself a dozen times that she had every right to make her own decision about who should repair the dents in her car, but the fact remained that she had become one half of a couple with Derek, and his half had somehow started overwhelming *her* half.

And yet she loved him. Sitting across the table from him, she could look at him and feel enormous affection for him, and there was no question in her mind about having made a very wise choice in her future husband.

But since Saturday she wasn't nearly as contented as she'd been, and that not only puzzled her, it angered her. On the flip side of those emotions, Blair felt a strong, defensive sense of self-sufficiency. For years she had looked after herself with few mistakes, and picturing herself as subservient to anyone, including a husband, was an abomination.

What she had to tell Derek should not be the major problem it seemed to be. She should be able to tell him anything, without fearing or dreading or worrying about his disapproval. And yet she had served his favorite dishes, as though deliberately trying to influence his mood.

She didn't like what she'd done at all. Purposefully she set her coffee cup onto its matching saucer.

"Derek, there's something we need to talk about."

"Sure, hon. What is it?"

He looked totally relaxed, his appetite sated, his mood mellow. She would treat the subject matter-of-factly, she decided. There was, after all, no logical reason for emotions to get involved in this discussion.

"I'm not going to bring my car to Duane for the repairs," she stated calmly.

Derek's eyes widened slightly. "You're not? But, hon, the car has to be fixed."

"It's going to be. Mr. Barclay has a friend who..."

"Back up here a minute, Blair. Barclay's the guy who ran into you?"

"Yes. Thorpe Barclay is his name, although he goes by Ace."

Derek shook his head. "I don't get it."

"You will, if you allow me to explain," Blair said patiently. "Mr. Barclay has a friend with the right tools and experience to make the necessary repairs. I agreed, today, to let Virge—that's the man's name—do the work."

"Blair, that's not a good idea. But it's not too late to revise your plans. I'm free in the morning. Let me take your car to Duane's and handle this thing in the right way."

Blair gave her head a slight shake. "Thanks, but I told Mr. Barclay he could have his friend do the work." At the impatience rippling across Derek's face, she added, "I can't go back on my word, Derek."

"In this instance I think it would be wise to do exactly that, Blair. Answer me this. What does Barclay have against Duane Kemp?"

"The arrangement has nothing to do with Duane's abilities or reputation. I told you on Saturday that Mr. Barclay has no car insurance, and he's..." Blair hesitated, because she didn't want to impinge on client confidentiality as far as Ace's application for a bank loan went. But Derek at least had to know of Ace's financial straits. "He's short of money," she finished evenly.

"And his lack of funds is supposed to move you?" Derek questioned somewhat sarcastically. "Blair, you're not being very sensible about this."

"I'd hoped you wouldn't disapprove," she said quietly.

"I more than disapprove, Blair. You've always been so levelheaded when it came to money. This isn't like you."

"I've also always been compassionate about anyone down on their luck, Derek."

"But compassion should only go so far."

Blair raised a cynical eyebrow. "And exactly how far is that, Derek?"

He flushed slightly, but Blair could tell his rising color was more from annoyance than embarrassment because she was questioning him about personal ethics.

This was the closest they'd ever come to an honest-to-gosh argument, she realized uneasily. They had so much in common, especially when it came to their single-mindedness about a financially secure future. For several years now she had thought of herself and Derek as being very much alike.

Apparently there were areas of outlook where they were miles apart, which was a sad fact to realize so close to their wedding day.

Derek was studying her. "Apparently this Barclay character has a way with words."

"Pardon?" Blair said, startled by the innuendo.

"How old is he?"

A sudden horrifying guilt made Blair defensive. "What difference does his age make?"

Derek's mounting anger further shocked Blair. "He talked you into this, didn't he? How'd he do it, Blair?"

"That's absurd, Derek. You're being unreasonable."

With anger distorting his features, Derek got to his feet. "You're the one who's unreasonable. Take a really good look at what you're doing, Blair, because I don't mind telling you straight out that I don't like it one damned bit!"

She could hardly believe this was happening. Derek's anger was genuine and chilling. Never could she have imagined a situation like this arising from such a simple disagreement.

And yet, deep down, she'd known—or at least suspected—that Derek wouldn't readily agree with her decision.

There was something silly and immature about fighting over who should repair her car, but there was nothing immature about the sudden fear gripping her vitals. Things had gone so smoothly for her and Derek that she'd never had reason to wonder how he would react to a show of independence from her.

If this was an example, heaven help them.

Blair slowly got up. "I'm sorry you see my decision as..."

"Stupid!" Derek interjected hotly.

Blair's eyes narrowed. A disagreement was one thing, but she would not tolerate name-calling. "Be careful, Derek. I don't deserve that nor will I accept that sort of behavior."

"Is this what I should expect after we're married?" he questioned harshly.

"If you mean, will I defy you, the answer is yes! We are not two people sharing one brain, Derek. I have as much right to my opinions and attitudes as you do to yours. Do you think I would ever treat you this way over a decision you had made on such an impersonal matter? What difference does it make who repairs my car?"

"I'll tell you what difference it makes! If that friend of Barclay's botches the job, do you think your insurance company is going to pick up the tab for a major face-lift? Not on a bet, Blair!"

"It's my car," she said flatly, stubbornly. There was a lot more at stake here than the cost of pounding out a few dents, dammit! She wouldn't back down now if her very life depended on it.

Thin-lipped and furious, Derek started for the door. "Call me when this idiotic mess is over," he yelled over his shoulder.

Stunned to her soul, Blair stared at the vacant doorway. From the front of the house came the slam of the outside door. She stood there for a moment, dazed. But then the thought arose: *This is ridiculous, crazy!*

Springing forward, Blair dashed through the house, calling, "Derek!" By the time she reached the front door, he was driving away.

Bewildered and slightly benumbed, Blair watched the taillights of his car disappearing down the street. It came to her then in a wave of incredulity that she'd never had occasion to cross Derek before. Was this how he usually reacted to a disagreement? How could one person believe so sincerely in another's even temper and be so wrong?

Blair felt the sting of tears in her eyes and batted her lashes to deny them. What good would crying do?

A tremendous longing for her brother struck her. She had any number of girlfriends who would be glad to offer sympathy, but her sad and upsetting story was apt to get around town and this wasn't a serious breach with Derek, it wasn't!

Going inside, Blair closed and locked the front door. After eyeing the living room telephone for a minute, she sat in a nearby chair and dialed Mitch's Seattle number.

When he answered, Blair's shoulders slumped with relief. "Oh, Mitch, I'm so glad you're home."

"What's wrong, Toad?"

Blair formed a shaky smile at the old nickname. As a youngster she had despised Mitch's choice of pet names, but tonight it sounded wonderful.

"Derek just left. He got terribly angry at me because..." Blair quickly outlined the incident. "What do you think, Mitch? Did I step on his toes without meaning to? Is it wrong for me to make any kind of decision on my own just because we're going to be married?''

"Well ... that's for you to decide, Blair. Derek's a pretty nice guy most of the time, but I remember a few incidents where he lost his temper.''

"But this is so silly.''

"You think asserting yourself is silly? Blair, you've never been a person to walk anyone else's line.''

"But we should be able to disagree and talk it out without losing our tempers.''

"Did you lose yours?'' Mitch questioned.

"Maybe a little,'' Blair admitted. "But not like Derek did.''

"And now you're scared.''

"I guess I am. The wedding's getting so close. My dress is nearly finished. The invitations have been sent. My bridesmaids are in the process of buying their dresses. The church has been reserved. And you've made plans to be here to give me away. What if ... oh, Mitch, what if I'm making a mistake?''

"Blair, if you have the slightest doubt, call it off.''

The drastic advice nearly floored Blair. She'd thought in terms of herself and Derek for so long, visualizing the future without him was staggering.

"I'm sure I overreacted tonight, Mitch,'' she said quickly with her heart beating so hard she could hear it. "Derek's probably trying to call me right now. How about if I call you back in a few days?''

"Do that, sis. Let me know what happens, okay?''

"Okay. G'night, Mitch. Thanks for listening.''

"Anytime, Toad.''

Four

Blair's telephone didn't ring that evening. Neither did she have a moment's peace. Pacing between rooms, stopping at windows to look out, worrying to the point of near nausea, she finally grabbed the phone at nine-thirty and dialed Derek's number. While it rang she bitterly denounced her actions on the car repairs and devised apologies.

But there was no answer at Derek's end. Frowning through eight rings, Blair slowly put down the phone. Where would he have gone, if not home? Or was he there and simply too angry to acknowledge her call?

That speculation seemed preposterous to Blair. One little argument couldn't possibly destroy their longtime relationship. How could he deliberately prolong an argument that had been irrational to begin with?

She called again at ten, at ten-thirty and eleven. She considered getting in her car and driving to Derek's duplex, which he had bought two years before. Living in one unit himself and renting out the other was extremely good business, he'd told her. "And after we're married and I move in with you, I'll have rent coming in from both units."

Blair began thinking of how often Derek used the pronouns *I* and *you*. There were instances when he said *we*, of course, but not when it came to money. Then it was *your* money and *my* money.

Her initial uneasiness over tonight's contention seemed to be growing into something huge and frightening, a monster that gnawed and clawed at her insides. If Derek had supposed his little tantrum would make her see how stupid she was and how intelligent and sensible *he* was, it wasn't working. Rather, Blair was thinking, remembering, questioning, and mostly about incidents that had gone right over her head at their time of occurrence. Discovering imperfections in the man she was going to marry in less than three weeks was a terrible jolt to the complacency to which she had become so accustomed.

When she finally went to bed a little before midnight, Blair's nerves felt close to being shattered. The tears she'd been fighting all evening came spilling out into her pillow while her emotions just seemed to get more tangled from the cave-in.

Throughout another several hours she anxiously searched for answers, and eventually fell into a deep, exhausted sleep, only to be jarred awake by her alarm at 6:00 a.m.

There was no flavor to the morning, which was a vast departure from the way Blair normally greeted a new day. Listlessly she got ready for work. The phone never rang, and her gaze was drawn to the silent instrument again and again.

A spark of pride wouldn't allow her to make another attempt to speak to Derek, and she left the house internally crushed because he hadn't called.

At ten-fifteen the telephone on her desk rang. "Blair Conover," she said dully. "May I help you?"

"Blair, this is Derek. Are you free to talk?"

"Yes," she said, nearly weeping with relief.

"Have you thought about what happened last night?"

"I've thought of little else, Derek."

"And?"

"And what, Derek?"

"Don't you have something to say to me?"

The apology she'd been so anxious to deliver last night was suddenly overridden by an overwhelming urge for complete honesty.

"Yes, I do have something to say, Derek," she said raggedly. "I think you were very unfair last night."

"I was unfair? What about you?"

Blair hesitated a moment, then conceded, "Maybe I was unfair as well, but . . ."

"But you don't believe I should have anything to say about how you might choose to waste your money."

His attitude dumbfounded Blair. "My God, Derek, do you really believe money's the issue in this problem? We disagreed over a decision I made. Disagreeing occasionally isn't abnormal for a couple, but becoming angry enough to walk out the way you did is going to extremes."

"You're not one damned bit sorry, are you?" Derek snarled in her ear.

Blair drew a shaky breath. "I can't believe you're acting this way."

"Tell you what, Blair. A little breathing space might be the best course for us right now. When you come to your senses, give me a call."

Trying to digest what was happening, Blair anxiously chewed on her lower lip. "Are you suggesting we don't see each other for a while?"

"That's precisely what I'm suggesting."

Blair was incredulous, stunned. He was actually going to punish her defiance by keeping them apart. Out of habit she had been watching the people in the lobby, and a customer was walking in her direction. "Someone's coming to my desk. I can't talk any longer. May I call you later?"

"Let's give it a few days, Blair."

She felt like bawling, but breaking down in the bank would cause a humiliating scene. "Very well," she whispered. "Goodbye, Derek."

Putting down the phone, she shaped a tremulous smile for the approaching customer. "Good morning, Mr. Laverty. Please sit down. I have your loan documents all ready for your signature."

As the day dragged on, Blair found herself on the verge of calling Derek a dozen different times. To think that a foolish argument could evolve into a trial separation was almost unbelievable.

But if she groveled now, what would Derek expect from her once they were married? He was wrong. Not that his being wrong guaranteed that she was right. But the issue wasn't who was right or wrong any longer, but how badly they had handled the first real controversy of their relationship.

Driving home that afternoon, Blair pondered the wisdom of keeping her word to Ace. Maybe there was no wisdom to it, she thought unhappily, but backing out of her promise to Ace would be too much like mindless obedience to Derek. And nobody on earth had the right to demand blind obedience from another adult, particularly when they were supposedly in love with each other.

She was beginning to wonder about love, about what it meant to one person versus what it meant to another, and it worried Blair that her feelings for Derek suddenly seemed so fragile. It wasn't possible not to resent his harsh, unrelenting attitude, nor to question the depth of his feelings for her.

What made it all so painful was how close they were getting to their wedding day. As she'd recited to Mitch, her and Derek's elaborate plans for a perfect wedding were in the final stages.

Deep down Blair knew if Derek should make an appearance or call with even a hint of regret, she would forget the whole awful incident. That hope gained prominence as she drove into her own neighborhood and then evolved into certainty that Derek would be waiting for her. But when her house came into view, her driveway and the street in front of it were vacant.

Sighing dismally, she left her car in the driveway and went in. Cooking anything was out of the question. For that matter, she was suffering from alternating bouts of jangling nerves and deep despair, and the only thing that made any sense at all was to get out of the house.

Changing from her business suit to a pair of old jeans and a T-shirt, Blair shoved her feet into canvas shoes, grabbed her purse and left the house. She drove to Houghton's one fast-food restaurant, ordered a plain hamburger and a soft drink at the drive-through window and then parked in the restaurant's lot to eat.

It simply wasn't possible to go anywhere in Houghton without seeing someone she knew, and after waving and yelling "Hi, how are you?" out the open window half a dozen times, she crumpled the remaining portion of her burger into its own wrapping and got out of the car to toss it into a trash container.

Feeling like a loose end and miserable about it, Blair departed the fast-food scene and headed out of town. The Consent of Liability form was in her purse. Leaving her car in Ace's hands would mean a good hike to and from work, but walking instead of driving for a few days wouldn't hurt her, and she truly couldn't abide the dents in her car.

She discovered, while traversing the back roads leading to what she still thought of as the "old Sutter place," that driving was therapeutic. The countryside was beautiful, still green and lush though there were drier summers in her memory when the grass had turned brown much sooner in the season.

Blair loved summer. Montana springs could be wet and cold, and autumns were totally unpredictable. Winter was her second-favorite season as she seemed to have an affinity for crisp cold air, and there were many winter days with brilliant sunshine though the temperature was below freezing.

But summer was special, which had probably added to her excitement about having a summer wedding.

Sighing despondently, Blair made the final turn onto the long driveway leading to Ace's ranch. It had been years since she had actually been on the place, but there'd been occasions to drive past it, and even from a distance the buildings had seemed dilapidated.

The place wasn't the same at all, she marveled. The buildings gleamed with fresh paint. The fences were straight and taut. Every speck of debris—the ancient, rusted pieces of equipment once visible from the highway—had been removed.

Parking her car next to Ace's blue pickup—the only vehicle in sight—Blair spotted him coming from the barn. She sat there and looked at him. Despite the present upheaval of her life, looking at Ace Barclay striding across the compound was a pleasure. He had a loose-gaited, almost-lazy walk. A sexy walk. This evening an old hat concealed his marvelous hair, and his jeans and shirt were vintage denim and chambray.

But the closer he got, the surer Blair became that his clothing was clean, as though he had changed in time for her arrival.

She got out and called, "Hello."

"Hi..." Ace bit back *sugar* and said instead, "Blair."

"You've done wonders with this place," Blair said as he walked up. With her fingers dug into the back pockets of her jeans, Blair's gaze admiringly swept the compound.

Blair Conover in a pair of snug jeans was a sight he might never tire of, Ace thought with a quick but thorough inspection of her long legs and firm, tight hips. And there wasn't too much wrong with the perky tilt of her breasts in that red T-shirt, either.

A light breeze was ruffling her hair. Blair let go of her back pockets and raised a hand to brush away some strands tickling her cheek. Ace's eyes narrowed in appreciation of one of the finest-looking women he'd ever been near.

"Would you like to take a look around?" he asked softly, almost praying she would agree.

"What?" Blair's gaze darted to Ace's blue eyes. "Oh, well, I guess there's no reason to hurry back to town. Sure, thanks, I'd love to look around."

They began walking toward the outbuildings. "I tore down two old sheds that were on the verge of falling down," Ace volunteered.

"The place looks great. Obviously you've done a lot of work out here."

"Me and ol' Virge."

Blair smiled. "Does ol' Virge live here with you?"

Ace laughed, because Blair's saying *ol' Virge* sounded funny. "Virge lives in the bunkhouse. He's gone right now. Gone most evenings, as a matter of fact. I think ol' Virge is in love."

Blair's smile vanished. "Well, I wish him luck."

Ace frowned slightly while he tried to decipher the strange tone of Blair's voice. He changed the subject. "We worked three days on bracing the barn."

"It's nice and straight now." She stopped walking to look back at the house. "I didn't remember the house as being so large." It was a squared-off structure, two and a half stories high, wood-sided, and with a porch wrapping itself around three of its sides. Quite a nice-looking house, actually. "Years ago I came out here for a birthday party. I think Johnny Sutter was nine or ten at the time."

Ace nodded. "I understand Johnny was killed in a car accident about five years ago."

"Losing Johnny nearly killed his parents, as well. From that day on, this place went downhill. I didn't know it was for sale, though."

"I don't think it was on the market very long before I bought it. Blair, would you like to see the inside of the house?"

She studied the sturdy old building. Mitch had come to the birthday party, too. There'd been at least fifteen kids, and several town mothers had hauled most of them out from Houghton. The party had been a rousing success, and recalling the happy occasion made Blair feel nostalgic.

"I think I would. Are you sure you don't mind someone snooping around your place?"

"Don't mind a bit. Come on."

Inside, Ace took Blair on a tour. The house was old-fashioned and charming, with tall, narrow kitchen cabinets boasting leaded-glass insets, hardwood flooring, high ceilings, and fireplaces with carved mantels. Without question it needed work. Like the outbuildings, the house had been neglected by the grieving Sutters.

But it had such marvelous potential, Blair found herself pondering paint and fabric colors.

"Want to see upstairs?" Ace questioned when Blair had inspected every room on the first floor.

"You're sure you don't mind?"

"Positive." Ace grinned. "I think you like this old place."

"It's wonderful, Ace, it really is."

"Come on." He took Blair by the hand and started up the stairs.

The sensation of the big masculine hand around hers hit Blair like a ton of bricks. She wondered how to withdraw her hand without looking like a hysterical female. But she couldn't bring herself to hurt Ace's feelings when he'd been nothing but nice since she got here. There'd been no smart-alecky remarks from him, nor any of those offensive endearments.

So she gritted her teeth and allowed him to hang on until they reached the second floor. At about the same moment Blair realized there would be only bedrooms and bathrooms up here, and she had no business snooping around Ace Barclay's house in the first place.

But there was still Ace's pride to deal with, which was completely apparent in his pleased expression as he opened the first door in the long hallway.

"There are four bedrooms—not all furnished—and two bathrooms, Blair."

She took a peek into the empty room. "Very nice."

The routine went on through four more doors, and she did take a few moments at two of them to admire the claw-footed tubs in the bathrooms.

But the final room was furnished and obviously Ace's bedroom. Instead of merely holding that door for Blair to see in, Ace walked to the center of the room and threw out both hands. "This furniture belonged to my great-grandparents."

The bureaus and bedstead were constructed of heavily carved, dark-stained wood bearing the patina of old age. From the doorway Blair's curious and surprised gaze moved from one piece to the next. For a second she almost laughed, because only a few days ago her opinion of Ace had him rootless and penniless. Penniless he might be at the present, but his roots obviously went as deeply as her own.

Blair's attention lingered on the bed. Easily, one could drape a canopy over the four tall posters, decorate with rich fabrics and colors, and turn this room into something special.

"I love it," Blair said simply.

"Do you really?"

She looked at the man who had initially impressed her as too cocky, too sure of his own appeal, and saw a little-boy expression on his handsome face. She questioned with some amazement, "Does it matter to you if I like your house?"

Ace took a step forward. "It matters."

The sudden heat in his eyes weakened Blair's knees, and she clutched at the doorframe. There was a heaviness in the air that hadn't been there a second ago, and she couldn't seem to do anything, not tear her eyes from Ace's or turn on her heel and get out of there.

Walking silently, he moved closer. At some point during the tour he'd gotten rid of his hat, which she only now realized. Her mouth felt cotton-dry, and she swallowed, searching for a moisture that simply wasn't there.

Ace hadn't planned this. He had never knowingly pursued an already-attached woman. But what he was feeling for Blair Conover was bigger than ethics. From the wide-eyed look on Blair's face, she was feeling the same thing.

Stopping within inches of her, he slowly brought his right arm up to encircle her waist. Her lips parted with a low moan. "No, Ace. No."

He brought her closer until her mouth was only a breath away from his. "Blair," he whispered huskily, and gently pressed his lips to hers.

In the next instant, gentleness vanished. Groaning deep in his throat, he threaded his hands in her hair and kissed her with unleashed hunger. He felt the exact moment when she began kissing him back, and then it was barely possible to think at all.

He couldn't seem to touch her enough, and his hands dropped from her hair to slide down her back to her hips and back up again. Beneath her clothing was soft yielding flesh, and all of the heat and response any man could hope for from a woman.

Blair was dazed and dizzy and lost in a never-before-explored world of sensation. His body was hard, his chest, his belly, his arms, his thighs. No man had ever kissed her with such abandonment. She ached from a desire with which she had no experience, and it didn't feel wrong. There was no voice in her head telling her to stop, or if there was, it was too faint to be heard above the roaring in her ears.

With his heart pounding like a crazy thing, Ace crushed her to himself. His lips were wet and seeking, demanding what a handful of wild kisses couldn't begin to satisfy.

Breathing hard, he began a stumbling movement toward the bed, holding her, kissing her, caressing her as they went.

Blair was on her back before she knew what was happening. She caught one brief glimpse of the smoldering heat in Ace's eyes before his mouth possessed hers again. Whimpering within the kiss because she realized they were on Ace's bed, she quickly lost even that small hold on sanity. Her body felt as though it had caught fire. An unfamiliar wanting was screaming through her system, making her writhe against the man causing it.

His hand slid under her T-shirt, and next the garment was drawn up over her head and tossed. They didn't speak. Her trembling fingers fumbled with the buttons on his shirt. Her bra was suddenly gone, and Ace's hot mouth and tongue tantalized first one breast and then the other.

When his shirt disappeared, Blair moaned and kissed his naked chest, nuzzling her face into the bristly hair upon it. Ace unbuttoned the waist of her jeans and worked them down while he kissed her until neither could breathe without gasping. She kicked away her shoes and then the jeans, and when he slid down her panties, she raised her hips to assist.

He kissed her belly, her inner thighs, the very essence of her femaleness. And it was as though her will had vanished with her clothes, because she let him go on and on and only craved more.

Then, with her lips swollen and her every nerve sensitized to the point of agony, she watched him sit up and remove his boots and socks. He stood up to shed his pants and briefs, doing it quickly, and returned to the bed to turn Blair and place her head on a pillow.

Ace stopped to look into her eyes, whispering hoarsely, "You're the most beautiful woman I've ever seen." He laid his hand on her breast, and she closed her eyes because the thrill of his touch made her dizzy.

His hand skimmed downward, and he kissed her lips, moving his tongue into her mouth to taste and tease. Her arms went up around his neck, and she held him with a sudden fierce intensity.

"Oh, Blair, honey," he whispered, and positioned himself between her lush thighs.

Blair was just barely aware of what he was doing. Nothing seemed real beyond the gnawing aches in her own body. No one had ever made her feel like this, so utterly devoid of moral restrictions. Ace's body was the most beautiful she had ever seen. He created an excitement she had never personally known to exist, and she wasn't thinking beyond this incredible moment. She couldn't.

Closing his eyes, Ace mated their mouths and then their bodies. Or, rather, he *attempted* to mate their bodies. Startled at what he was feeling, he raised his head and looked Blair in the eye.

"Tell me you're not a virgin," he said gruffly.

She closed her eyes and licked her lips. "You're not a virgin."

"Don't play games, Blair."

Her eyelids lifted slowly. "Don't stop, Ace."

"Do you know what you're doing?" Christ! What the hell kind of idiot was she planning to marry? Letting a sexy, sensuous woman like her walk around unloved was nothing short of criminal!

"No," she whispered. "But you've made me want to know."

He couldn't ask about her fiancé, not at a moment like this. He wanted her so much he hurt, and she wanted him. *Him!* Why, if she loved another man enough to marry him, did she want Ace Barclay?

Blair's fingertips rose to his face. He could see the glassy desire in her eyes and knew he'd caused it. "No other man ever made me want to know," she whispered.

That did it. Stopping was no longer an option for Ace, though if she had said anything at all about this being a mistake, he would have hopped off this bed and taken a cold shower to cool off.

There was some anger in the sudden hard thrust of his body, and he watched Blair's face crumple in pain. His heart nearly stopped from remorse, and he kissed her sweet, trembling lips. "I'm sorry, honey. It won't hurt again, I promise."

Perspiration had broken out on her skin, but even the stinging pain hadn't destroyed the desire gripping and controlling her. "Do it," she whispered brokenly. "Do it."

He went easy, though he couldn't remember a time when he'd wanted to let go more. He wanted to roar and shout, and rush to completion, to take his own pleasure and to hell with hers.

But he couldn't do it, not with Blair. He felt her deep inside of himself, in a place no other woman had ever touched. And there was no reason to hurry. This would be the end of her engagement to a guy who had to be the biggest jerk of the century. He would have a hundred, a thousand opportunities to teach her each and every one of the joys of making love.

"Open your eyes, honey," he whispered. "Look at me while I'm loving you."

"No." She kept her head turned slightly and her eyes closed. The sensation of his body sliding in and out of hers was incredible, much more exciting than she had ever imagined making love to be. His weight was wonderful. The texture and heat of his skin had her mesmerized.

And that magical maleness at the base of his belly was God's greatest creation. Did Ace think the same about her?

Her hands moved over his muscular upper arms and shoulders while he moved within her. "You're fascinating," she whispered.

"And you're the most amazing woman I've ever met," Ace growled. She wouldn't look at him, but from the play of emotions on her face, she was riding the same wave he was on.

He looked at her tangled taffy-and-sunshine curls on the pillow beneath her head, and the sweep of her long lashes against her flushed cheeks. A feeling of possession had him gritting his teeth. She was his. Not just for today, but for all the days to come. Not in a million years could he have suspected her virginity, but to think that no other man had made love to her had Ace soaring.

She began moving with him, her hips rising and falling with his. "Oh," she gasped with each thrust.

"Is it good, baby?"

"Oh, yes...yes. *Yes!*"

He felt her shuddering release. She cried out and dug her fingernails into his back. He held nothing back then, and shouted her name a minute later.

Exhausted and drained, he collapsed and laid his head on the pillow next to hers.

It took Blair a long time to recover. For minutes her body seemed almost paralyzed with the most delicious peace she had ever experienced. Remnants of that final perfect moment echoed in her system until she frowned at the dim light in the room and realized the sun was going down.

Without warning, Derek's face flashed into her mind. "Oh, my God," she whispered. "What have I done?" Her voice rose to a nearly hysterical volume. "Get off of me! How could you do this to me?"

Five

Shocked and doubting his own hearing, Ace brought his head up. "What did you say to me?"

"Let me up, Ace," Blair moaned. Her hands rose to shield her face, but not before Ace saw her misery.

His heart was suddenly hammering. "Blair, we didn't do anything wrong."

"Get away from me!"

"You're blaming me," he said incredulously.

Blair's hands jerked away from her face. "Well, who else would I blame?" She squirmed and pushed at him. "Get off!"

His eyes narrowed. He wanted to hold her there, to shake some sense into her, to show her how easily he could make her want him again.

Instead, angrily, he rolled to the bed. She scooted away immediately and tried to cover herself with the edge of the bedspread. Disgusted, Ace got off the bed and walked out.

The second he was gone, Blair jumped up and began looking for her clothes. She was shaking. Her vision was blurred by tears. She had lost her mind with Ace, and the damage was irreparable. She would never forgive herself, never!

Nor would she forgive him. He had ruined her life. He was exactly as she'd thought on Sunday, an opportunist, a damned gunslinger!

He was only gone a minute, returning to the bedroom wearing a towel around his hips. His lips were set in a thin, grim line, and he stood there watching her struggling into her jeans with a bitter taste in his mouth.

"What's this all about?" he finally asked harshly.

She sent him a look designed to kill. "I never want to see you again. Is that clear enough?"

He felt stabbed to the quick and flinched from the pain. "Blair, don't do this."

Grabbing her shoes in her hands, she started for the door. Ace intercepted her and took hold of her shoulders. "Dammit, don't you dare walk out of here without talking to me!"

She tried to shake off his hands, but he only held on tighter. "Ace, let go of me!"

"Not until you talk to me."

Blair tried to glare and ended up crumpling. Ace caught her and brought her to his chest. Her canvas shoes thumped to the floor. "What's wrong, honey?" he murmured with his lips in her hair.

"I . . . didn't want this," she said on a sob.

He pushed her back to see her face. "I didn't force you, Blair."

"But you turned me into someone else." Her voice rose with a hysterical note. "I have nothing to give my husband now!"

"My God, you have more to give than any woman alive. But you can't marry that other guy." Ace's eyes were dark with emotion. "We belong together. We're special." He brought his mouth down and kissed her, hot and hard.

It took Blair a moment to realize she was kissing him back, that she was clinging and moving against him, and that her body was suddenly alive and pulsating with desire. Again.

Shocked, she tore free of his arms and backed up to a wall. "Do you actually believe I'm going to repeat the worst mistake of my life?"

"There's too much chemistry between us for pretense," Ace said low. "You'll repeat it, and so will I. Every chance we get."

Wild-eyed and breathing erratically, she stared at him. The towel around his hips had slipped some, exposing the line of hair on his belly that she knew led to his manhood. She had thought him thin at their first meeting, but his leanness was merely taut masculine skin over sinewy masculine muscles. His hair was mussed and falling over his forehead, and he was, in a word, utterly gorgeous.

Biting her lip, she held her stomach and moaned. "I...can't do this. *I can't!* Derek..." Horrified, she stopped to moan again.

So the guy's name was Derek. Ace's features tensed. Blair's misery created an ache in his gut. He didn't know how to deal with such anguish. Never had he made love with a woman and been faced with something like this after it was over. He thought of reminding her that he'd tried backing off and she hadn't let him, but he couldn't be that cruel.

There was more to Blair's innocence than what he'd discovered a few minutes ago on his bed. In his experience, there weren't very many of her kind of woman walking around. He remembered his smug thoughts about this being the end of her wedding plans and almost laughed, albeit cynically. What the past thirty or so minutes had accomplished was to plunge them all, Blair, himself and that jerk, Derek, into an emotional morass. And the whole damned mess was complicated by their arrangement about Blair's car and his application for a bank loan.

Turning away, Ace cursed under his breath. Snagging his briefs and jeans from the floor, he showed Blair his back and dropped the towel to get dressed.

Seemingly glued to the wall, Blair watched through the mist of tears in her eyes. Her mind shrieked, Why? Why him? Why had she eluded Derek's advances, certainly anything beyond kisses, and then given everything to a man she barely knew?

Gunslinger or not, she thought unhappily, Ace was a unique person. He was probably accustomed to women making fools of themselves over him, but why? What did he have that Derek did not?

For the first time Blair was aware of the points of soreness in her body. Her breasts felt tender and there was discomfort between her legs. Ace had hungrily, passionately sucked on her nipples, wetting them with his tongue. He was a big man, and his weight and penetration during the final act had left his marks on her.

Dredging up the events on his bed to tie them to the aches she was now feeling, Blair moaned and turned away from the sight of Ace yanking on his clothes. She could do it all again with him, experience the rushing need, the pleasure, the ultimate bliss. What kind of woman was she to be engaged to one man and want another?

She felt Ace's hand on her back and took a deep, shaky breath. "Please don't touch me."

He left his hand where it was. "Come on. I'll drive you home."

Turning with astonishment, she said, "Surely you don't think I'm going to leave my car here after this!"

"Why wouldn't you? The car needs fixing and you agreed to Virge doing it. Making love didn't change anything, Blair."

Her eyes widened. "It changed *everything!*"

"Not everything," he said evenly. "Let me tell you what it did change." He tapped her chest with his forefinger, just above her left breast. "Because you loved what we did, something in here will never be the same. You'll think of me whenever your blood heats up, and make no mistake, sweetheart, it *will* heat up again. You'll compare Derek's kisses to mine. You'll find yourself comparing his ways to mine, and the little things, like how he moves, what his attitudes are..."

"How could I compare attitudes? I certainly don't know how *you* feel about anything!" Blair scoffed, if in a weak and tremulous voice. But he was right about her comparing kisses; she'd already been doing that.

"I'd be glad to rectify that oversight anytime you say the word," Ace said bluntly. His eyes narrowed. "Stay the night with me. By morning you'll know everything there is to know about me."

Stay the night. Sleep with him in that big bed and experience, again and again, the rapture of being under him. Feel his kisses and the heat of his palms against her skin, the sinfully exciting pleasure of him exploring the most secret portions of her body.

But her reality wasn't this most charming of rooms in this wonderful old house. Her reality was in Houghton, in her own house, at the bank, in seeing Derek again and making amends, somehow. In facing him while suffering the guilt and the agony of the damned.

"I can't, and please don't suggest anything like that again," Blair said wearily. "If you're ready to drive me home, let's go."

"Then you're leaving your car here?"

"Yes, but only because I don't have the strength or the ability right now to figure out another solution."

"Blair, I'm not going to leave you alone, if that's what you're thinking. This isn't the end of it for us."

"It's the end as far as I'm concerned," she said bravely. "Please... let's go."

Tight-lipped, Ace led her to the first floor and through the house to the back door. Outside, Blair detoured to her car without saying anything, and for a moment Ace thought she had changed her mind and was planning to drive away on her own.

But she came out with her purse and car keys. Ace walked around his pickup and opened the passenger door for her to get in. He couldn't think of anything to say to make her feel better, and deep within himself was too much satisfaction at having found Blair to let his conscience start acting up. He climbed behind the wheel thinking that maybe he should feel like a dog for having taken what rightfully belonged to a man named Derek, but there was a personal euphoria in his system that precluded any such self-denouncement.

He cast her a glance as he got the truck turned around and headed for the highway, and saw only the back of her head as she gazed out the side window.

It was getting dark. Ace switched on the truck's headlights. After a few minutes of heavy silence Blair went into her purse for a paper.

"This is that form I told you about."

"I'll sign it at your place."

"And the keys to my car." Blair laid both items on the seat between them. "I need the car on Saturday."

"I know. Virge'll start working on it in the morning." Ace sent her a glance. "I don't want us parting like this. You're mad at me and you shouldn't be."

"Fine," she said dully. "I'll forget you and take my anger out on myself."

"You're not going to forget me. Stop kidding yourself."

"Think what you want, but believe me, I'm going to do everything in my power to forget you. And this evening."

"And you're going ahead with your wedding plans as though tonight didn't happen?" Ace questioned sarcastically.

"I...don't know what I'm going to do." Derek would know, she thought wildly. He would take one look at her guilty face and know everything!

But if by some slim chance he didn't, could she pretend an innocence she no longer possessed? Lying had never been easy for her. Her mother had laughed every time Blair had attempted to fib about some misdeed as a child. *Honey, don't ever take up acting as a career. The truth is always written all over your pretty little face.*

Maybe lying didn't come easily because she despised lies, and if Derek and she still had a future together, she couldn't see herself guarding a guilty secret for the rest of her life. The only alternative, confessing to Derek what she had done with Ace today, made her heart flutter alarmingly and her breath come in short gasps. Her hand rose to the base of her throat as the tears started again.

Ace frowned in her direction and caught on that she was crying. Muttering a curse, he jerked the truck to the side of the road, turned off the motor, moved her car keys and the insurance form to the dash, and slid across the seat. Without waiting for permission, he pulled Blair into his arms and cradled her head against his chest.

"Tell me about it," he whispered. "Talk to me, honey."

Her fingertips curled into his shirt. "You don't understand."

"You're probably right, but don't you see what we've got?"

She jerked away from him. "We've got nothing! I've known Derek almost all of my life. How long have I known you?"

"Is that how you measure feelings, how long you've known a person?"

"You've probably never even been close to love and marriage. How would you know what I'm feeling?"

"Don't tell me you love Derek, Blair. I don't care how many plans you and he have made together. If you loved him, you wouldn't have responded to me. It's that simple, babe. A happy and sexually contented woman doesn't seek another man's bed. Old Derek let you slip away, honey, and that's his problem, not yours. Just be thankful that you found out *before* the wedding, because I'll tell you something, Blair. If you and I had met afterward, the same thing would have happened between us."

She gasped. "You're crazy!"

Ace nodded. "Crazy about you." He lifted a hand to her hair, though she tried to elude it. "I can't even ask if you've ever made love in a battered old pickup, can I?" he said softly. "Do you know what it means to a man to be a beautiful, exciting woman's first lover?"

"It's what you've stolen from...Derek," she whispered, shaken to her soul because she actually *wanted* him to go on touching her.

"I'm not a thief, honey. You gave me a gift, I accepted it. And I'll accept it every time you offer."

She inched closer to the door, afraid of the power he had over her senses. "You're crowding me. Please move over."

"Tell me what you're going to do about Derek," Ace said quietly. "I want to see you again and soon."

"No! Can't you at least try to understand?" Losing sight of everything but how necessary it was that he comprehend and accept her dilemma, Blair grabbed his hands and held them. "Ace, promise you won't try to see me again. Promise!"

He looked at her in the dim light. "I can't promise that, Blair. Don't ask." Untangling their hands, he slid his down to her elbows and then up to her shoulders. "Let me kiss you," he whispered hoarsely. "Let me do what we're both aching for."

She'd had just about all of the emotional upheaval she could take for one day and began shaking like a leaf in a gale. "Take me home, Ace. You've already caused enough trouble between Derek and me."

He gave her a quick shake. "What're you talking about? What trouble?"

She was just upset enough to tell him. "He's angry because I agreed to let your friend repair my car instead of taking it to the garage."

"He's angry at you? What is he, some kind of moron?"

"He's not a moron, damn you! He's . . . he's . . ."

"He's a jerk," Ace muttered. "And stupid, to boot. Any man who doesn't make damned sure his woman gets so much loving she never even looks at another man has rocks for brains."

"I wouldn't let him! He wanted to. He's as normal as you are, but I always said no!"

"You said no to him and yes to me. Doesn't that tell you something? Blair, you don't love him. Can't you see that?"

"I *do* love him! For God's sake, don't construe what you and I did as love."

"I didn't say it was, did I? But it was a hell of a big step to something important, Blair. That's all I'm telling you. Just don't throw it out without giving it a chance."

Her shoulders slumped, and she didn't even care that his hands were still gripping them. "Either take me home or drive back to your place so I can get my car. I don't want to be with you any longer, Ace. I'm exhausted and sick to my stomach."

Because she was crying again, Ace let go of her. But he only sat there and looked at her. "I think you've got a lot of soul-searching to do, Blair. Personally I don't give two hoots about Derek, but even a jerk doesn't deserve a wife who would rather be sleeping with someone else. Give that a little thought, sweetheart," he advised coolly as he slid over to the driver's seat.

Blair wept quietly during the balance of the drive to town. She dug tissues out of her purse and used them to sop up the tears, but they just kept coming. By the time Ace pulled into her driveway, her eyes felt puffier and more swollen than her lips. She knew she had to look like the wrath of God, and she sent silent thanks heavenward that Derek hadn't decided to come by and wait for her to get home.

As soon as the pickup stopped she reached for the door handle. "Blair...wait."

She turned her head to see him. "There's nothing more to say. Call me when my car's ready." Quickly she got out and gave the door a push to close it. She was halfway to the house when she heard Ace's door open and shut.

But he didn't come after her or say one word. As she went in she saw him standing next to his truck, just watching.

Her house felt like a sanctuary. She stood in the dark and absorbed its familiar smell and the sensation of security it always gave her.

Ace's truck started. Blair squeezed her eyes tightly shut and listened. When the motor sound faded to silence, she unerringly walked through the dark house to her bedroom. It wasn't late, she saw by the lit clock on her bed stand, barely ten. But she was too torn up to do anything beyond taking a hot bath and going to bed.

Placing her purse on the dresser, Blair got out a fresh nightgown and made her way to the bathroom, where she finally turned on a light.

The sight of her face in the mirror shocked her. Her hair looked like it had lost a battle with an electric mixer. But while her eyes were as swollen and red as she'd thought, her mouth looked only soft and plump. It looked, she amended uneasily, as though she'd been well kissed.

Which she had. Her jaw clenched while she studied her reflection. A certain kind of knowledge was dangerous. Sexual power was a lethal weapon. Ace had both.

Whatever Ace did or didn't have, she was a fool. Nothing would ever be the same again. She couldn't marry Derek without a confession, and with a confession he probably wouldn't marry her. What man would?

All of her plans, her perfect wedding, the wedding night that was going to be so special, the honeymoon—she had traded it all for a roll around Ace's bed.

Blair winced. Relegating her response to a "roll around Ace's bed" was horrible, but what else should she call it?

How had it happened? How could a woman who had lived with the highest moral standards for twenty-four years, a woman who had sensibly eluded horny boys in high school and more than a few horny men after that, suddenly lose every ounce of her self-respect and do what she did this evening?

Ace deserved a lot of the blame, true, but he was, after all, only a man. One of Cheryl Conover's pieces of advice during girl-talk sessions between mother and daughter had been, *You can't blame a man for trying, Blair. It's up to the woman to say yes or no. Remember that.*

Blair had taken that advice to heart. This evening in Ace's bedroom, where she'd had no damned business being, she could have said no. *Should* have said no. What was so devastating was that merely thinking about the episode on Ace's bed made Blair's body feel hot and heavy. Ace had said her blood would heat up again and that she would think of him when it did, because she had loved how he'd made her feel. *Loved* it! How did he know so much more about her than she, herself, did?

Groaning, Blair laid a hand over her eyes. Nothing in her life had prepared her for this painful situation. Far better for her if she hadn't clung so tenaciously to virtue and was experienced enough to take tonight in stride, or at least, put it in some sort of bearable perspective. The awful truth was that her strict morality had never before been really tested. Ace had administered the test and she had failed it, abysmally.

Sighing heavily, Blair finally got the water running in the tub.

A half hour later, feeling slightly better, the water was gurgling down the drain and she was drying off. The ringing of the telephone gave her a start. Uncertainty bombarded her again, and she stood there and let it ring.

But it didn't stop ringing. Wrapping the bath towel around herself, she went to her room, sat on the bed and reluctantly picked up the phone. "Hello?"

"Where in hell have you been? I've been calling all evening."

"Derek," she said weakly. "Uh ... I was ... out."

"Out where?"

"Please don't question me like that. I'm tired and was just going to bed."

"At ten-thirty?" he snarled as though she stayed up much later as a matter of course.

Another inane argument was in the making and she wasn't up to it. "Derek, did you call for a reason?"

"Do I need a reason to call my fiancée?"

"But you told me not to call you."

"Blair...I might have been a little hasty about that." His voice had changed, becoming softer. "I miss you, hon."

Instead of elation or happiness, or even satisfaction because he was ready to forgive and forget, Blair felt only a yawning emptiness. Love for any member of the male species, other than her brother, seemed miles away.

Her voice turned cool. "I think you were right, not hasty. Let's leave it at that for a few more days."

"What? Blair..."

The panic in his voice didn't move Blair. "We don't know each other as well as I thought, Derek."

"I know you, Blair."

"No, Derek, you don't. I'm not sure I even know myself anymore."

"You're still angry with me."

"I was never angry with you, Derek. *You* were angry with *me,* don't you remember? I don't want to argue about it. Let's say good-night now."

"Blair..."

"Good night, Derek." Blair put down the phone and drew a slow, unsteady breath. Eventually she had to tell Derek everything, but not tonight. God, not *tonight!* she silently repeated, on the verge of tears again.

Getting up to bring the towel to the bathroom, Blair put on her nightgown and returned to her room and bed. She settled down in the dark with a long-suffering sigh, and then lay there and thought of living out her life without any man. There was comfort in the exercise. A dignified, quiet lifestyle looked vastly more appealing than the highs and lows she had undergone during the past few days.

The next fifteen minutes were used up in a painful depiction of canceling her wedding. She had already received some gifts, which would have to be returned. Her dress had to be paid for, whether she ever wore it or not. The cake could be easily canceled, but at least one of her bridesmaids had already purchased her dress and would have to be reimbursed.

The worst part, of course, would be calling everyone she had invited and explaining that the wedding was off. Derek could call his friends and do his own explaining, but unquestionably the good citizens of Houghton would have something to talk about.

And then, as though waiting all along for his turn to haunt and pester, Ace's image appeared in Blair's mind. Thorpe Wilson Barclay, gunslinger, rancher, lover, the man who had ruined her life.

Blair frowned. Or was Ace the man who had set her free from girlish inhibitions? Her pulse rate picked up. Undeniably she was a different woman tonight than she'd ever been. Was the person she was right now really that terrible?

Derek would think so, once he learned the truth. Ace thought she was sexy and beautiful. What would Mitch think if he ever knew? He had told her to call off the wedding if she had even one doubt, she remembered, so Mitch probably wouldn't judge her one way or the other.

And did anyone else's opinion really matter? Other than her own, of course. For that matter, how she viewed herself was undoubtedly the most important consideration.

Blair was still pondering the subject when the phone rang. It had to be Derek calling again, she thought. He probably couldn't believe her attitude and intended to talk her out of it.

He wasn't going to talk her out of anything. No one was ever going to make decisions for her again. Sitting up, Blair turned on the lamp and picked up the phone. "It's getting late. Why are you calling again?"

"Blair?"

The strangest thrill rippled through her vitals. "Ace. I thought it was someone else."

"Derek?"

"Don't mention his name to me again, Ace. I have no intention of discussing Derek with you on even the most impersonal level. Why are you calling?"

"To find out how you are. Are you okay?"

"No, but I don't plan to discuss that with you, either."

"Don't be so cold with me, Blair. I care..."

"You care about yourself, Ace. You're a poacher, a damned gunslinger, and..."

"I'm a what?"

"You heard me."

Ace chuckled in her ear. "I ain't aiming to go after old Derek with a shootin' iron, honey."

"That's not what I meant and you know it. You wanted me and you came after me, without giving one thought to the consequences."

"You wanted me, too."

"I never would have made the first move!"

"How about the second?" Ace asked softly.

Goose bumps popped out on Blair's skin. Even his voice affected her. She clenched her jaw. "Good night, Ace. Please don't call me again."

After slamming the phone down harder than necessary, Blair snapped off the lamp and pulled the covers up to her chin. She squeezed her eyes shut and wished for her mother.

And that was something she hadn't done in a long while.

Six

Wednesday passed uneventfully, for which Blair was immeasurably grateful. After walking home from work she went into her house and spent a quiet evening. When the phone rang—three different times—she ignored it.

On Thursday she told herself she felt stronger, and that she would have that necessary heart-to-heart with Derek during the upcoming weekend. The wedding was only two weeks away, and she couldn't put off the awful task indefinitely.

She was at her desk, working on a loan-settlement statement for a customer, when she became aware of being watched. Looking up, she saw Ace seated in one of the extra chairs at Winona's desk. He nodded. Blair nodded back—an involuntary reaction—and then immediately lowered her eyes to the papers in front of her.

But her insides suddenly felt like quivering jelly, maybe because she hadn't expected to look up and see Ace. Whatever the reason, concentrating on numbers was impossible.

It was as though there were a flashing beacon over there at Winona's desk, and Blair wanted to drop all pretense and just stare.

The sensation alarmed her. The feelings Ace aroused were not appreciated or wanted, but she seemed to have no control over them. She stole a furtive glance and registered him and Winona laughing together. Apparently, Blair thought peevishly, even a fifty-year-old grandmother wasn't immune to Ace Barclay's brand of charm.

What seemed so threatening to herself was that she couldn't seem to hate Ace. She could resent him, and she did, she could wish that he'd never come to Montana, or even been born, but she couldn't hate him.

Neither did she feel any animosity for Derek, although, getting down to hard facts, this whole nasty business could be his fault. If he hadn't been so mean about her car, he might have gone to the Barclay ranch with her on Tuesday evening, which would have prevented any and all foolishness between her and Ace.

She was still looking for someone to blame, Blair realized with a disgusted grimace. And laying what she'd done on somebody else's shoulders was only wriggling away from the contemptible truth: she could have said no and hadn't. It was that simple.

From the corner of her eye she saw Ace getting up. He lingered for another few words with Winona, then started ambling Blair's way. Her heart was suddenly in her throat, and she ignored his advance until he was standing right in front of her desk.

Praying she looked nonplussed, she raised her eyes. "Yes?"

With a slight grin Ace leaned forward. "Don't use that prissy tone on me, sugar. Remember I've seen you with your hair down and your skin all flushed and dewy."

Blair's eyes narrowed while she raged, "Don't you dare talk to me like that in here."

Ace leaned closer. "See me tonight, Blair."

The sensual expression in his eyes stopped Blair's breath in her throat. "I . . . can't," she whispered.

"Yes, you can. Since you're on foot I'll come to your place."

"No! Ace, I'm warning you . . ." Blair became aware of Winona's curious stare. "People are watching. Leave me alone. I know you have to come to the bank because of your loan, but you don't have to single me out like this."

"Honey, you just naturally stand out all on your own." Ace straightened his back. "See you tonight."

A terrible picture of him beating on her door loud enough to rouse the neighbors brought Blair out of her chair. "Wait!"

Ace turned. "Yeah?"

"I . . . I'll meet you somewhere. I don't want you coming to my house." For once and for all, she thought, she was going to get it through Ace Barclay's stubborn head that she wanted nothing more to do with him.

Ace's gaze moved down her pale blue dress and then up to her face again. "You look fantastic. Where do you want to meet?"

Blair tried to think. "Uh . . . there's a small park near my house. I'll be there at . . . after dark."

He wanted to point out how much more sensible it would be for her to simply get in his truck and drive out of town if she didn't want to be seen with him.

But he only nodded. "Fine. See you then."

Casting Winona a sheepish smile as Ace walked away, Blair sat down and feigned enormous interest in the loan-settlement statement before her. Tonight she would explain herself very clearly to Mr. Gunslinger Barclay, and at some point of the coming weekend, she would explain herself to Mr. Overbearing Kingston. All in all, she'd just about had her fill of male superiority.

The hike home from the bank felt good to Blair that afternoon. Except for the dark clouds overhead that had appeared rather suddenly, the seventy-five-degree weather was perfect for exercise.

She just might leave her car at home from now on, she thought at her front door, amending the idea to exclude stormy days. Walking in, she heard the telephone ringing and tossed her purse on a chair to answer it.

It was Derek. "Blair, this little misunderstanding has gone far enough. I'm coming over after my class tonight. I'll be there around nine."

"I won't be here," she said coolly and quickly.

"You're going out?"

"Yes," she replied without explanation.

"I drove by the bank today and your car wasn't in its usual parking place."

"That's because it's being repaired at Ace Barclay's ranch."

"You really gave it to him to fix? Blair, that's the most stu—"

"If you dare to call me stupid one more time, Derek, I swear I'll—" She cut off the threat. "Just don't do it."

"You've changed, and I'd like to know why."

"I'd like to see you on Saturday, Derek."

"I thought you were going to Billings on Saturday."

"My plans are different now. Will you come to the house on Saturday?" Blair bit her lip as a wave of apprehension tore through her. Envisioning that confession was like receiving a blow to the belly.

"If I didn't have a tutorial session with the Hastings boy, I'd come right now. But you won't be any later than I will, will you? You can't be going very far without a car. Couldn't I come over when you get home?"

"I don't know how late I'll be."

"Then tomorrow evening."

"Saturday," Blair repeated with some acerbity.

"I don't understand this, Blair."

"You will. Goodbye, Derek."

She couldn't muster up any sympathy for Derek, nor did she plan to endure any for Ace when she talked to him at the park. In a strange way the two men were lumped together in her mind, both of them giving her a bad time although using diverse tactics. She was balking at the pressure and not ashamed of it, either.

Blair changed from her working clothes into an old denim wraparound skirt and a red checked blouse. The phone rang and she ignored it, which she knew she couldn't keep on doing. Other people called besides Derek and Ace, after all.

She made herself some supper, relying on canned soup and a cheese sandwich. She read the newspaper and did the crossword puzzle, and realized throughout that the uninterrupted peace was soothing to her jangled nerves. It was a condition she planned to reinforce, even if it meant she never so much as spoke to another man for the rest of her life.

Blair did a load of laundry and a few chores in the house, on edge about meeting Ace in the park but determined to set him straight. As darkness settled in she saw the first raindrops on the kitchen window.

In minutes it was a downpour. Blair opened the back door and looked out. The park was only in the next block, but it was suddenly pitch black and very wet out there. She closed the door and thought, Now what?

She didn't have long to wonder. As though on cue someone rang her front doorbell.

It would be Ace, of course, she thought irritably as she hiked through the house. He was probably tickled pink that it had started pouring at the very time she should be setting out for the park.

She yanked the door open and said at his amused expression, "This is not funny!"

"If you don't want me in your house, come for a ride with me," Ace said logically.

Anything was better than inviting him in, Blair reasoned. "I'll get a sweater. Wait here."

Ace huddled beneath the narrow roof over Blair's front stoop. She'd left the door ajar, and after a minute of dodging gusting rain he stepped inside.

The living room was directly to the right of the small foyer. Ace looked in and found the room uncluttered and nicely decorated.

Blair returned and instantly stiffened. But it was pouring outside, so she made no comment about Ace standing in her foyer. "I'm ready."

They ran for Ace's truck. Only, when Blair got there she saw a van instead. Ace yanked open the passenger door and she climbed in, then he hurried around the front of the van and got in himself. "Damn, this is some hard rain."

"You never said anything about owning a van."

Ace started the motor and flipped on the heater. "It's ol' Virge's." He sent Blair a grin. "He didn't go courtin' tonight so I borrowed it."

Blair looked behind the individual front seats and saw a bed. *A bed!* She swiveled around to face front again so fast Ace nearly choked.

"It's ol' Virge's playpen, not mine," he reminded as he backed out of the driveway.

"Then why did you bring it instead of your truck?" Blair said tartly. The van began moving down the street slowly, its windshield wipers sweeping rain from the glass.

"My truck broke down. Remember we were going to meet in the park, Blair. I never thought you'd even see the inside of this van."

"You had something in mind, Ace. Don't try to convince me otherwise."

"I'm not a liar, Blair." Ace made a left turn.

"And all you wanted to do tonight was talk," she said sarcastically.

"Isn't talking all you want to do? Let's lay our cards on the table, Blair. If you want more, I'm your man. But talking seems pretty important to me right now. I've been trying to talk to you since Tuesday night, but you're either gone a lot or you're not answering your phone."

"Both," she muttered. "I haven't wanted to talk to either you or..."

Ace sent her a curious glance. "You're not talking to Derek?"

"I asked you not to mention his name."

"You brought it up, not me."

The van made another left turn and Blair questioned, "Where are you taking me?"

"Not far. Just relax."

But she knew Houghton too well to relax. The road they were on led out of town to the old rock quarry, and while discretion was wise in this meeting, it wasn't necessary that they go to the most secluded spot in the area.

"Go back to the park by my house," she demanded.

"Will you please relax?"

"Said the spider to the fly," Blair muttered, drawing a laugh from Ace.

Rain was coming down in sheets, putting the wipers through their paces. Visibility was poor and Ace drove without haste. Blair didn't exactly relax, but there was something calming about the rain on the van's roof, the low purr of its motor and the warm air coming from its heater.

"Blair, honey," Ace said softly. "Would you like some music? Ol' Virge's got quite a collection of CDs in that box behind your seat."

"I do not want any music," she retorted. "And I wish you'd park somewhere so we can get this over with."

"In a hurry, huh?"

"Your innuendo is duly noted, but that's as far as it's going."

"So you're completely immune to me? You don't even know I exist? I could be some guy you never made love with and you wouldn't know the difference?"

"Drop it, Ace."

The van stopped abruptly, and Blair peered out into the drenched darkness to vaguely make out the barren configuration of the old quarry. No one had crushed any rocks out here for years, and there'd been talk around town, off and on, that the place would be treacherous if it ever filled up with water.

It hadn't, and nobody that Blair knew paid the slightest attention to the area's posted No Trespassing signs. The quarry, in fact, had become a favorite necking spot for teenagers. If there was another vehicle out here tonight, though, Blair couldn't see it.

Ace turned off the motor. "Are you warm enough?"

"I'm fine." Blair turned in her seat to see him. "There's only one reason I'm here, and that's to tell you point-blank to stay away from me."

"I think you already did that," Ace drawled.

"But you don't believe I meant it. You think you can strut around and . . . and flirt, and act like God's gift and I'm going to fall at your feet, or something. Well, I'm not. I don't know how to tell you any plainer, and . . ."

"Take a breath, Blair. You're getting awfully excited."

"Don't make fun of me, Ace. Until you exploded into my life, everything was great. Now . . ." Her voice cracked.

"Now what, honey?" Ace prompted softly. "Is ol' Derek giving you a hard time? Did you tell him about us?"

"Damn you, there is no 'us'! And . . . I'm going to tell him on Saturday," she added lamely.

"Good. He should know."

"Oh, you're so smug I can't stand the sight of you!"

All signs of levity vanished from Ace's system. "If I really believed that, you'd never have to set eyes on me again. But you're lying, Blair, if not to me then to yourself. What I'd like to know is why you're fighting the feelings between us so hard. What's wrong with you and me being together? Why is Derek acceptable and I'm a—what did you call me? A gunslinger, wasn't it? I'm not sure what you meant by that, but it wasn't intended as flattery, was it?"

"No, it wasn't intended as flattery," Blair confirmed dully. "It's what we used to call a guy on the make in high school."

Ace sucked in a sharp breath. "And that's how you see me, as a guy on the make?"

"What do you expect after those horrible *honeys* and *sugars* you tossed around?"

"You don't like being called honey?"

Blair's eyes flashed angrily. "You brought up the word *flattery*. Do you think being treated like a tramp is flattering to a woman?"

"Good God, I never treated you like a tramp! Maybe I got a little out of line when we first met, but you're a damned good-looking woman. Don't tell me other guys haven't tried to make time with you, Blair."

"Gunslingers have," she said pointedly.

The windows were steaming up, and Ace cracked his about an inch to let in some fresh air. "I don't think I like that word."

"Because the shoe fits."

They sat there in silence for a tension-laden stretch. Finally Ace spoke. "What do you call Derek?"

"Pardon?"

"If he's not a gunslinger, what is he?"

Blair took a breath. "I thought he was a gentleman until recently. Now I don't know. Frankly, I'm sick of men in general."

"Because one made a woman out of you? Or because one made you, period. What did you want to do, die a virgin?"

"I was going to be married, damn your hide!"

"Yeah, that's right. You were going to marry ol' Derek, a guy who apparently has better things to do with his hands than touch the woman he supposedly loves. You should be thanking me for saving you from a cold and emotionless future, honey. Let me point out that neither of us was cold or emotionless on Tuesday night." When Blair didn't make an immediate reply, Ace added, "And I don't feel so cold and emotionless right now, either. Just seeing you, being near you, makes me want you, Blair.''

Blair felt like a steel band was tightening around her chest. She couldn't deal with Ace wanting her, and ignored the comment entirely. "Derek isn't . . . cold. He's just . . ."

"Just what, Blair?"

"He cares about my feelings!" she blurted.

"Yeah, he sure does. Didn't you say he got royally ticked because you made a deal with me about your car repairs? Sounds to me like he lies awake nights worrying about your feelings."

"And I suppose you'd be any different with a woman?"

"With you, I would."

Blair's head was beginning to ache. "Let's go back to town," she said wearily. "This was a waste of time. No one, especially a woman, is going to tell the great Ace Barclay what to do."

"That's not true." Sliding from the driver's seat, Ace knelt in the aisle next to Blair. It was so dark, neither could make out the other's features, but his gaze rested on the blurred oval of her face. "Take my hands, Blair."

"No!"

Though she tried desperately to elude him, Ace found her hands and took hold of them. "Listen to me, Blair. Tell me you don't want me to kiss you. Say it like you mean it. Make me believe it and I'll take you home and never bother you again."

She was suddenly choked and hoarse. "I . . . don't want you to kiss me."

"You didn't convince me. Try again."

"This is absurd," she whispered raggedly.

"You can't do it, can you?" He brought her hands to his face and placed one on each of his cheeks. "Don't you know what's happening with us, honey?"

"No," she admitted in a weak, emotion-clogged voice. "And don't tell me your version, please. I can't handle any more pressure right now."

"You're unhappy, and that tears me up," Ace whispered. He turned his head slightly to place a lingering kiss in the palm of her hand.

Blair shuddered and pulled her hands back. "Please don't do that."

Ace sat back on his haunches. "Blair, all I'm asking is that you see me."

"Don't lie to me, Ace. I might be green, but I'm not stupid." She winced at the word, because it seemed to get more insulting every time it came up. Never could she have believed Derek would use it on her, and he'd done so twice.

"All right, fine. We both know I want more than friendship from you. Our biggest problem is that you want me in the same way and refuse to face it."

"That's your ego talking," Blair scoffed. "Take me home, Ace."

He hesitated for a long moment, then climbed into the driver's chair. He looked at Blair while he started the engine. The headlights flashed on, and he kept looking because he could see her now.

She finally looked back, and the same clutching tension that had thrown her into Ace's arms in his bedroom was between them again. His eyes looked black in the dim light, the angles of his face more pronounced. His wide shoulders cut the darkness, as did his big hands on the steering wheel.

"You didn't convince me about not wanting my kiss," Ace said with a challenge in his low voice. "Feel like trying it again right now?"

Swallowing the lump in her throat, Blair forced her eyes forward. "Take me home."

"You are one stubborn lady," he said softly. "What're you planning to do, get rid of both ol' Derek and me?"

"It's a thought."

"You're not cut out to live without a man, Blair. And I'm not talking about a guy who's satisfied with a sappy goodnight kiss when you're hot to trot."

Blair sucked in a sharp breath. "You're crude."

"I could be a hell of a lot cruder." Ace's temper was heating up. He turned on the windshield wipers and slammed the shifting lever into Drive. "I'd like to romance you, Blair. I'd like to do all of the silly, mushy things men do when they're head over heels for a woman. But you won't meet me even a tenth of the way, and you know what I think? I think it's because of Derek, the damned fool! He led you to believe that a woman shouldn't feel what a man does. Or what some of us feel, at least. You're scared spitless of a genuine, honest-to-God sexual relationship with a man, which is what we've got. Us, Blair, you and me. Or what we *could* have if you'd ever get past your—"

"Stop it!" she screamed. "Just stop it! Who do you think you are? You barged into my life and changed everything! Yes, Derek is upset with me about my car, but he wouldn't have any reason to be angry if you hadn't run into me! And don't demean something you know nothing about. I'm sure the only relationship you understand is one that . . . that wallows in mud. Well, I don't happen to like mud, and neither does Derek. We were completely happy with each other until you came along!"

"And now you're not. If that doesn't tell you something, I'll be damned if I can." Ace stepped on the gas and got the van moving. He drove with his eyes on the rain-drenched road, every bit as furious as Blair.

Their tempers had cooled by the time they reached the Houghton town limits. Blair sat stiffly, but she had learned a great deal tonight—about Derek, about herself, and yes, about Ace. This wasn't over, not by a long shot. She was going to face Derek on Saturday with the complete truth, and if that was the end of their plans, so be it.

As for Ace, denying that he affected her physically would be the biggest self-delusion of her life. But sexual desire and love were two different things entirely. Among everything else Blair had learned from tonight and the past week, that was the most meaningful. The ideal relationship, of course, would contain both elements.

Which she would get from neither Derek nor Ace. She had, Blair decided, finally grown up.

The pole lights on her street barely penetrated the density of rain and darkness. Blair honestly never saw Derek's car. Ace pulled the van into her driveway and left the motor running.

"Here's that insurance form," Ace said, handing it to her. "You forgot it last night."

Blair took it. "Thanks."

"Let's not part in anger," he said quietly.

"Even though anger is what you're feeling? Ace, I'm not going to see you again."

"I know you're not. I hope you're happy, Blair. I want you to be happy. Obviously Derek's won. I wish you the best, honey. I mean that."

Her mouth went dry. "Thank you. My car—?"

"Will be ready on Saturday morning as promised. I'll have Virge bring it by. I'll have to come into the bank every so often, but I won't bother you."

There were suddenly so many tears in her throat, Blair could barely speak. "Good night, Ace."

"Want me to walk you to the door?"

"No, I can manage. I left lights on all over the place." Blair opened the door and slid to the ground. "Goodbye, Ace."

"Bye, sugar. See you around."

Blair ran for the house, though the rain seemed to be lighter now. She went inside and the van drove away. It was, she thought, the end of the evening.

But a cynically taunting voice from the living room archway shocked her. "You've been with Virgil Potter. That was his van you just got out of."

"Derek! How did you get in?" She had never, ever given anyone a key to the house, not even Derek.

"The back door wasn't locked. Don't bother lying about this, Blair. I know Virgil Potter's van."

Poor ol' Virge's reputation was on the line right now, but Blair was too upset over Derek lying in wait for her in her own house to worry about anything else.

"I told you I'd be out," she said coolly.

"I won't put up with this kind of behavior," Derek said with an expression of utter domination.

Blair looked at him and felt the last remnants of the feelings she had construed as love for him dying a surprisingly painless death. "You're absolutely right."

He backed up a step. "Wait a minute."

"No, you wait." She removed the engagement ring from her finger and held it out. "Take it. It's over, Derek. I'm going to cancel everything in the morning."

"Because of that fat tub of lard, Potter? Blair, have you lost your mind?"

"Not because of anyone else, Derek. Because of you. Instead of asking me where I was tonight, you thought the worst. You judge whatever I do, Derek, and I don't want to be judged anymore, not by anyone. Marriage between us wouldn't stand a chance." She dropped the ring into his hand. "I'd like you to leave now."

"You're going to regret this, Blair."

"I don't think so. I'd like to say one thing, Derek. You were there for me when my mother was ill and after she died, which I will always appreciate. My mistake was in interpreting gratitude and friendship as love. You don't love me, Derek, any more than I love you."

"We've said it often enough."

"Yes, we have. Is it possible for us to remain friends?"

His face became ugly right before her eyes. "You're a cold bitch, Blair, and if it's friendship you want after this, go to someone else. I'm going to be busy looking for a real woman."

Her mouth dropped open, but Derek was already out the door and didn't see it. Trembling suddenly, Blair pushed the dead bolt and then hurried to do the same with the back door. She turned out lights and sought the comfort of her bedroom.

All along Derek had thought of her as a "cold bitch." Why had he asked her to marry him? Had he hoped she would thaw and invite him into her bed long before this?

She had cheated him . . . and herself. There were better things in store for both of them.

But in her case, "better things" was not going to include Ace Barclay. And he was the only dark and handsome stranger she had met this summer.

It seemed, Blair thought with some cynicism, that Madam Morova was full of . . . beans.

Seven

Ace found out about the canceled wedding by accident, during the week just prior to the Sunday the ceremony was supposed to take place. He was in the post office to buy some stamps and there was a short line of patrons ahead of him. Two young women immediately in front of him were chatting about this and that, when one, a redhead, said to the other, a brunette, "Did Blair call you about her and Derek canceling their wedding?" Ace pricked up his ears.

The brunette nodded. "Yes, I guess she's called everyone by now. I wonder what happened."

The redhead leaned closer to her friend. "I have no idea, but Derek's already seeing someone else."

"Who?"

"Marie Layton."

"No kidding? That's awfully fast, isn't it? Do you suppose he and Marie were chummy before? No, forget that. I can't say anything against Marie. She's a nice gal even if it does seem awfully quick for Derek to be dating another woman. Is Blair dating anyone?''

"Not that I know of."

For the first time Ace felt a true remorse. If not for him, Blair would be going ahead with her wedding plans. Maybe she did tell Derek what happened at the ranch.

Still, remorseful or not, there was just the tiniest glimmer of elation in Ace. Logically speaking, Blair couldn't have been in love with Derek. She'd been closer to love with him than she'd been with her fiancé, or she never would have kept Derek at arm's length and made love with him.

The two emotions, remorse and elation, battled for prominence throughout the next few days for Ace. As the days stretched to weeks, he gave the matter less thought and really only felt a repeat of the disruption when he went into the bank and saw Blair. Which only happened twice, as the only time Ace went to Houghton Security was when Winona called and needed more information from him to process his loan.

The wheels turned slowly at Houghton Security, Ace had discovered. Even after Winona called with the news of the loan committee's approval of his application, the delays— all logical, all necessary—seemed interminable. Ace had sold two steers at auction to pay for the upfront costs of the loan and to exist until he had access to the bank's money. But those auction funds wouldn't last indefinitely, and he didn't want to start depleting his herd every time he needed a few bucks.

He was working hard at the ranch, he and Virge, and poor ol' Virge hadn't been able to draw a paycheck for nearly a month. Ace was anxious for the loan to close so he could get his operation functioning on an even keel.

Blair wouldn't allow herself to dwell on the breakup. There were times when the question arose about just how much affection beyond ordinary friendship had been between her and Derek when the first small disagreement caused so much trouble, but mostly, Blair took each day as it came and tried not to analyze the past.

The times that Ace came into the bank were always like a physical blow, however. His polite nod in her direction upset her, and Winona's giggling like a teenager because of something Ace had said was just about the most annoying thing Blair had ever witnessed.

Maybe what really irritated her was that Ace had gotten off scot-free. Obviously she was just another easy mark to him, which hurt more as time went on. But she and Derek had paid an awfully big price for Ace's intrusion in their lives, while Ace was going blithely on about his business.

Rationally Blair knew Ace hadn't caused the breakup. Actually, as Ace had so crassly pointed out, she should probably be thanking him for saving her from a marriage that couldn't possibly have brought anything but unhappiness for both her and Derek. But every time she saw Ace sauntering into the bank with his cock-of-the-walk strut and that gunslinger grin on his face, she *wanted* to blame him.

The day Ace came in to sign his final loan papers, Blair was standing at the copy machine. Running copies, of course. A whole slew of copies. Instantly that just-punched sensation delivered a wallop to her system, and there was a moment when she actually felt dizzy.

She frowned. Weird spells of dizziness had been hitting her even when Ace *wasn't* in the vicinity, and for about a week now, in the morning, she'd had to deal with completely unreasonable bouts of nausea.

She felt the blood draining from her head as a horrifying thought took shape—*What if I'm pregnant?*—and she hung on to the copy machine to keep herself upright and steady.

Dear God, I only did it once! She began to count frantically, much too frantically to make sense of time and the calendar. She glanced at Ace and received one of his maddening nods, for which she repaid him with a glare of pure venom. She saw his startled reaction and turned away, trembling suddenly.

Blair's truly dirty look pained Ace. He scrawled his signature wherever Winona pointed on one paper after another without reading any of them, wondering all the while why Blair had decided to hate him again.

"The amount of your loan is now at your disposal, Ace," Winona declared with unmistakable pride at the good job she had done him and the bank. "Would you like any or all of the funds transferred into your checking account?"

"Only five thousand today," Ace said absently while getting to his feet.

"I'll take care of it. Wait for a deposit slip," Winona said as Ace wandered off.

"I will." Ace headed for Blair. He'd left her alone as he'd promised, but that murderous look needed some explanation. The copy machine was behind a hip-high railing, and he rounded it with his jaw clenched. "Blair?"

She whirled. "You can't come back here! This area is for bank employees only."

"I'm here, and I'm staying till you explain that I-wish-you-were-dead look you just threw at me."

Nervously Blair glanced around. Naturally Winona was keeping close tabs on the scene, but Winona wasn't the only one. Mr. Hendrix, the bank's general manager, happened to be in the lobby and was eyeballing the whole thing, as well.

"Do you want me to lose my job?" Blair hissed under her breath.

"All I want is an explanation."

"I'm not explaining anything to you in here."

Ace took a look at his watch. "It's almost closing time. I'll be waiting outside." Ace strode around the railing and back to Winona's desk. "Got that deposit slip ready?"

"Here it is." Winona held out the slip. "Ace, I don't mean to intrude, but it's a strict rule of the bank that employees cannot have personal callers during business hours."

"No problem," Ace said smoothly. "If there's one thing I respect, it's a strict rule. Thanks for all you did to get me that loan, Winona. See you around."

When Ace was through the front door, Winona got up and walked over to Blair, who was trying to concentrate on the zillion copies flipping out of the machine. "Blair, are you all right?"

"I'll live," Blair said in a weak stab at humor.

"That Ace is quite a character, isn't he?"

Blair couldn't think of a response. Ace wasn't just a character, he was the father of her baby, *if* she was pregnant. Too befuddled to even pray it wasn't true, she gathered up the stack of copies with unsteady hands. Smiling feebly at Winona, she mumbled something about needing to get these filed away before closing time and made a beeline for her desk.

Outside, Ace leaned against the front fender of his truck and watched the side door of the bank. Employees began trickling out a few minutes after five. Winona waved at him and got into her car, and then, finally, Blair walked out.

She was clutching her purse to her chest. She saw Ace push away from his truck when he spotted her, and then put his hands on his hips. His belligerent stance irritated her and she had half a mind to ignore him completely, jump in her car and drive away.

But what if it was true? What if the worst had happened and she was pregnant? Was she strong enough to face the town with a baby and no husband? It happened occasionally, although it was a rare event in Houghton, and there was gossip and snickering, make no mistake.

It wouldn't be fair to the child, not in a small town like this. Options flew around in her brain, everything from leaving Houghton and going to Mitch in Seattle, to abortion, though the mere thought of abortion made her skin crawl.

Lifting her chin, she headed across the parking lot to Ace. "What do you want?" she asked, neither tactful nor friendly.

Ace's eyes narrowed. "What makes you think I want something?"

"Don't you?"

"Only an explanation of that poisonous look you gave me in the bank."

Blair swallowed and felt panic riffling her spine again. She wasn't thinking clearly, except for one painful thought: it wasn't fair that women paid such a high price for a moral misstep and men did not. Ace had moved her sexually, the first man who ever had, and she had forgotten everything, who she was, the standards by which she had lived her life, her promises to another man.

Ace sensed something peculiar going on behind her dazed eyes. "Blair? What's wrong?" When she didn't answer, he took her arm and leaned closer to her. "Blair?"

"I...I think I'm..."

"What? I didn't hear you."

"...pregnant."

Ace heard that just fine. He didn't move, just held on to her arm while they both stood there like a couple of statues.

Then, as though coming awake, Blair gave her arm a sharp shake, throwing off his hand. "Wait just a damned minute," Ace growled as she turned and started running to her car.

She was almost in it when he grabbed her. "Leave me alone!" she yelled, then regained enough sensibility to look around. Nearly everyone had gone; the parking lot was close to vacant. She took a deep breath. "Don't look so panicked. It's too soon to know for sure."

"I'm not the one who's panicked," Ace retorted. His eyes bored into Blair. "Can you drive all right?"

"Of course I can drive all right," she snapped.

"Then get in and go home. I'll be right behind you."

Sick at heart, Blair slid behind the wheel. It was a little late to be wishing she hadn't spoken so heedlessly, but wish it she did, all the way home.

She had no idea what to expect from Ace, nor what he might expect from her. Bravely she went into the house, aware of him right on her heels. Inside, she tossed her purse to a living room chair. Ace stood in the doorway, staring with an expression she saw as grim.

"What do you want to do?" he began bluntly. "Get married?"

Blair's mouth dropped open. "Don't be absurd."

"And don't you start thinking I've got nothing to say about this. If you're pregnant, it's my baby."

Something perverse made Blair drawl sarcastically, "What makes you so sure of that?"

Ace's complexion changed color, taking on the dark hue of deep anger. "Don't plant foolish doubts, Blair. This isn't a kid's game."

"I'm as aware of that as you are, believe me."

"Why are you so mad at me? Because I made you pregnant? We were both careless that day, wouldn't you say?"

Blair's emotions were beginning to drain her. Why in God's name hadn't one of them had the sense to worry about protection? Wearily she turned away. "I don't even know if it's true. Let's leave it at that until I find out for sure."

"That makes sense. But if it is true, what're we going to do about it?"

"I . . . don't know."

Ace moved across the room and stood behind her. "Blair, please think about getting married. I think we'd stand a good chance of making it work."

She turned. "Based on what, Ace, the fact you ran into my car, or because we went to bed together?"

He looked stunned. "That's a rotten remark."

"It's an *accurate* remark! Do you know me? Do I know you? How much time have we spent together? I don't even know if you have any family. We'd be two strangers diving into a very serious relationship, and you think we'd stand a good chance of making it work?" Blair shook her head. "I don't think so."

"What's the alternative, you having the baby alone?" Ace's eyes took on a harsh gleam. "Unless... Tell me you're not considering abortion."

She studied the signs of revulsion on his face, the frustration, and felt her first glimmer of compassion for the male's role in childbirth. Though of an unquestionably dissimilar nature, maybe men paid just as high a price as women for moral laxity, she thought unhappily.

Relenting, she said quietly, "Abortion isn't an option as far as I'm concerned."

Ace heaved a relieved sigh. "You had me worried for a minute." Looking at Blair, he felt that old tug of desire. Maybe there was a lot they didn't know about each other, but he felt they connected in the most crucial way for a couple. "Will you think about marriage?"

"I'm sure I will," she said tonelessly.

"Let's go out for dinner and talk about it." Ace managed a grin. "I've got some money now. My loan closed today."

She took a moment to think, then shook her head and moved some distance from him. "Not tonight. The idea of a...a baby is brand-new to me, and I need some time alone to digest it." Honesty made her add, "I wish I hadn't said anything to you about it."

"Meaning what? Let me tell you something, Blair," he said with some sarcasm. "No kid of mine is going to be raised without his father."

"Oh? You already have practical experience with 'kids'?" she said frostily.

Ace's mouth thinned. "If I did, I wouldn't be ashamed to admit it to anyone. But no, until now that particular experience has escaped me. As for your wondering about my family, I have a brother who's married with two young sons in Colorado. Jack and I inherited our folks' ranch fifty-fifty, but we don't always see eye to eye on how to do things, and we decided that one of us had to buy the other out. That's what happened. Because Jack has a family, we decided I should be the one to leave. That's how I got the money to buy the Sutter ranch.''

So he was raised on a ranch. In Colorado. And he had a brother, a sister-in-law and two nephews. Somehow having a family gave him substance, a clarity that had been missing before. Blair suddenly felt the strangest confusion. Since meeting Ace—Thorpe Wilson Barclay—she had judged him entirely on her lack of knowledge. He'd shown her a cocky veneer, which was maybe only skin-deep, maybe not, but there was just possibly more to him than she'd been thinking.

It was distressing to realize at this particular moment that Ace's strong physical magnetism hadn't abated an iota. She could wonder and worry about his determined involvement in this phase of her life and still feel him in that seemingly isolated sector of sensuality that he had liberated within her.

But marriage? And a shotgun marriage to boot?

As though taken by an unexpected chill, Blair wrapped her arms around herself. "I didn't bring up your family to pry."

"Are you feeling all right?"

"I'm . . . tired."

"Blair, will you call me after you see a doctor?"

"Uh . . . yes." What else could she do? And maybe calling him would make better sense after a few days.

"You're sure about not going out to eat?"

"I'm sure, but thanks for asking."

There was a ponderous ache in Ace's midsection. Seeing Blair unhappy and upset—*worried*—wasn't a pleasant feeling, especially when he had caused it. He should have kept his head that day. He should have left her alone when he discovered she'd never been with another man. The fact that he'd changed her life completely wasn't something he could ignore any longer.

"I'm sorry, Blair," he said quietly. "Sorry for everything. You'd be married to Derek if it weren't for me."

The one thing she didn't need right now was sympathy, and just as she feared her eyes began filling. Ace saw her tears and felt them in his own soul. Closing the gap between them, he pulled Blair into his arms, with his big hand holding her head to his chest. She resisted, then gave up. It felt good to be held, and Ace's embrace was probably only meant to be comforting.

That *was* all Ace intended, to soothe her at this troubling moment. But she was so warm and womanly, and it wasn't but a minute before his body began reacting to her scent and softness. He closed his eyes and gritted his teeth. A pass right now wouldn't be wise. Blair's mood was far from romantic. Her mind was cluttered with worry, and he could tell she was trying hard not to cry.

But damn, she affected him! She had from the moment he'd set eyes on her, driving along in front of him with her eyes on everything but the road. He'd seen blond tangled curls in the car ahead, then a pert profile, and God knew Ace hadn't been paying much attention to the road, either.

That collision had started one hell of a chain reaction, Ace thought grimly with a long-drawn breath and an inching closer than was smart to the woman in his arms. But he felt a small snuggling movement from Blair, and his pulse went wild.

She was merely seeking solace, he told himself, but his left hand slowly skimmed down her back to curl around her waist and bring her closer still.

Blair knew what was happening and couldn't seem to stop it. Her breath seemed stopped, though, in the center of her chest, and her tears were drying at a remarkable speed. The languid, heated sensation in the pit of her belly was far more influencing than the small voice in her head telling her to back away, to break this up before it got out of hand again.

Ace tipped her chin and looked into her eyes. "Let's make this work, Blair," he whispered, and brought his mouth down to cover hers.

The touch of his lips weakened Blair's knees. His mouth opened, urging hers into the same configuration. His tongue slipped between her lips and she suddenly felt smothered by her own desire.

Breathing roughly, she broke away. "Not today, Ace."

He was shaken by her denial of the passion between them. "We're both free now. Why not?"

Blair winced. "A reminder that I wasn't free before isn't going to persuade me." She leveled a hard gaze on him. "I'd like you to leave."

Ace hesitated, not really considering doing anything but what she asked, yet not exactly eager to do so, either. "We're connected, Blair, even without the baby. Let down your guard, honey. I'm not going to hurt you."

She walked from the living room to the small foyer and opened the front door. Ace trailed along. "You're a stubborn woman, sugar," he said cockily to conceal the sudden sharp pain he was feeling. To prove to them both he could take it, he flicked the collar of her blouse with his forefinger in a carefree gesture. "Call me as soon as you see a doc, okay?"

Blair's nod was brief and without any of the emotion tearing her apart. When Ace was through the door, she closed it silently and slid the lock into place.

Three days later, Saturday morning, Ace was on the phone. "I've been waiting for your call."

"I couldn't get an appointment," Blair lied.

"Next week, then?"

"My doctor will be gone next week."

"Can't you see someone else?"

"I could but I'm not going to," Blair said evenly.

"Only one doc will do, huh?"

"He's been my doctor for years."

"Well, I guess I can understand that. In the meantime, will you let me come over?"

"Why?"

Ace gritted his teeth. "To see you. To talk. And don't tell me we have nothing to talk about."

Since her appointment with her doctor in Billings and hearing his verdict, Blair had been going through an unusual transformation. Out of a strange and newfound strength, she was seeing the future in a vastly different light than she ever had. She would probably marry someday, but it would never happen for the wrong reasons, and rushing to the altar with Ace because she was pregnant would definitely be a mistake. When her condition became too obvious to keep private, she would face the town, her employer and anyone else who dared to judge her.

There was really only one person whose opinion mattered anymore, and she had already tried calling her brother and planned to keep trying until she caught him at home.

As for Ace, she felt absolutely no guilt about lying to him at this point. Eventually he would learn the truth, everyone would. But these first few months were her own. Hers and the small life's in her womb.

"We have only one possible area of common ground," she told Ace calmly. "So, I disagree with you about needing to talk."

"Don't shut me out, Blair. I care what happens to you."

"Because I might be carrying your child?"

"There are other reasons."

"Maybe because I was so easy. What are you thinking, Ace, that I..."

He cut her off. "Don't say it, Blair!"

"Fine, I won't say it, but I'm thinking it."

What hurt was that Ace couldn't deny that Blair was right on the money. He couldn't think of her anymore without thinking of sex, without remembering the excitement of their one time together, without reliving it to the point of arousal.

He was aroused right now, and it was frustrating as hell when he knew—*knew*—he could bring her to the same feverish pitch if she'd just give him the chance. This had to be more than a normal attraction between a man and woman, because it was about to drive him nuts!

"I stayed away because I thought you'd chosen Derek," he said with some anger. "But you didn't choose him, you canceled your wedding. I'd like to know what the problem is now, why you won't give me the time of day."

"I'm the first to admit making more than one mistake in my life," Blair shot back. "I just don't plan to make any more."

"You go right for the jugular, don't you?"

Blair's shoulders slumped. It was a gorgeous day outside, and she was inside and participating in a no-win argument. "Ace, please. I need to be left alone."

"Well, you're not going to be left alone! There's a chance you might be pregnant with my baby, and I'm not going to stay out of it, Blair."

"What happened to 'sugar'?" she asked bluntly. "You're like every other man, Ace. A woman is sweet as long as she's doing exactly what some man wants. Well, listen to me, my friend. This woman is going to do what *she* wants for a change, and if anyone doesn't approve, tough toenails!"

Blair carefully fit the phone onto the receiver and walked away from it.

Eight

On Sunday afternoon Blair had a caller. She opened the front door with surprise all over her face. "Derek!"

"Hello, Blair. May I come in?"

Blair had heard about him dating Marie Layton and truly didn't care that he'd found a "real" woman so quickly. But she honestly couldn't imagine a reason for this visit after his nasty parting remarks at their last meeting.

"What for, Derek?"

"I just need to talk to you. Please, Blair. It won't take long."

She frowned slightly, realizing that he looked as if something was seriously bothering him.

Relenting, she stepped back. "All right." She brought him to the living room and gestured to a chair. "Sit down, if you like."

"Thanks."

Blair sat on the sofa, directly across from the chair Derek had chosen. He leaned forward, his forearms on his knees. "The way we...uh, parted has been needling me, Blair. You didn't deserve what I said, and I'd like to apologize."

Blair's unswerving gaze took in his blond hair, slender build and the tiny squint lines at the outer corners of his eyes. Derek was a nice-looking man, she decided again. And some of her old, old affection for him was still present in her system.

But what had ever made her think she was in love with him? They went back a long way, granted, clear to childhood, but longevity had very little to do with the kind of love that made a relationship exciting and permanent. Hadn't Ace pointed out something to that effect?

"Thank you," she said quietly, introspectively.

"Maybe you've heard I've been seeing Marie Layton."

Bringing herself back to the immediate present, Blair nodded. "If the relationship is important, I wish you both the best."

"That's good of you, thanks."

Blair sat back with a logical "There's really no reason all of us shouldn't remain friends."

"I'd like that, Blair." She saw him squirm a little. "Uh...Blair, what I really wanted to say was..." He hesitated and grinned weakly. "It took me a little time to realize it, but I guess what I'm trying to say is that we were never right for each other."

"I know," she said softly.

Obviously relieved, Derek nodded. "Thought you might. Are you seeing anyone? I hope you are, Blair," he quickly added so she wouldn't misunderstand.

That was when Blair began worrying about false courage. Sitting here right now with Derek, was she capable of telling him of her condition and that she wasn't planning to marry the baby's father? As time passed, that was exactly what she would have to do and not only once. The story would have to be repeated again and again, to her employer, to friends, to her pastor.

To her brother. She'd been trying to reach Mitch for exactly that purpose, but uncertainty had returned and now she wondered if she really had the courage to do so.

Her situation felt like an unsolvable dilemma again, she realized unhappily. Her lips formed a smile for Derek, but it was as phony as a three-dollar bill.

"No, I'm not seeing anyone," she told him.

He got to his feet. "Well, I'm sure you will." His right arm rose to offer a handshake.

Standing herself, Blair accepted the peace offering. "Thank you, Derek," she said quietly. "I appreciate your coming by like this."

"'Bye, Blair."

She walked him to the door. "Goodbye, Derek."

After he'd gone, the relief she felt was inarguable evidence of the turmoil she had been living with. At least now they could run into each other and say a civil hello. The idea of friction between them had been gnawing at her, apparently.

As far as Derek went, Blair understood him and herself much better. Their relationship had never really passed a certain point, and they had both striven to make it more. Of course it hadn't worked. How could it? No one could force the special feelings it took to make true lovers of a couple.

Her quandary now lay solely with Ace. Was her attitude with him too harsh? Even aside from the fact that any decent man had a right to his child, was she too concerned with how she and Ace had met, and the changes in his personality whenever he wasn't completely confident?

He resorted to flippancy whenever self-assuredness deserted him, she knew now. And when had she become so judgmental? So censuring? Weren't those the very qualities she had objected to in Derek?

That evening Blair took care of her usual Sunday-night ironing and pressing, all the while eyeing the phone and contemplating that call to her brother. But she was no longer eager to impart her news. Burdening Mitch with a problem he could do nothing about was really very cowardly on her part. What had she been hoping to hear Mitch say, that he approved? He wouldn't, Blair knew, although she also knew he would stand by her.

It was just too soon for such candor. When she ultimately related her impending motherhood to her brother, she should also have a plan for her and the baby's future well in mind to soften the blow.

She looked at the phone again, although not with any further thoughts of Mitch. It was Ace in her mind now, and the small life in her body. Her future included Ace in some capacity, however she might prefer keeping him out of it.

But she wasn't all that sure about keeping him out of it, Blair realized uneasily. She wasn't sure of anything anymore. Only a short time ago every phase of her life had been planned and, she'd believed, satisfying. Meeting Ace Barclay had disrupted longtime patterns and certainly her own contentment, but resenting him to the point of trying to pretend he didn't exist was immature. Especially with the enormous relief she felt about *not* marrying Derek.

It struck her then: she had to give Ace a chance. He didn't know the baby was an actuality, nor did he have to know it yet. If she tried and he tried and nothing happened, then she could regather her courage and go on from there.

Walking to the phone before she could change her mind, Blair dialed Ace's number. He answered after the second ring, sounding sleepy.

"I hope I didn't wake you," she said with a frowning glance at her watch. It was only nine-thirty, but she didn't know Ace's habits.

"I came to bed early. Don't worry about it. I'm glad you called."

So he was in bed. A mental image of him, hair tousled, warm and sleepy-eyed, caught Blair off guard, and a sudden breathlessness made her seek a nearby chair.

Small talk escaped her completely and she got right to the reason for the call. "I was wondering if you'd like to come for dinner tomorrow evening."

"Do you have news?"

"News? Oh, no, nothing like that," she said quickly as comprehension hit her. He was asking about the baby again.

In his bedroom, Ace sat up and snapped on the lamp. An invitation from Blair coming out of the blue like this wasn't to be taken lightly. "Yes, I'd like to come," he said into the phone calmly, though his eyes were squinted in speculation. "What time?"

"Around seven."

"I'll be there." Whatever was going on with Blair, this call was exciting for Ace. Maybe she had finally come to grips with the potent feelings between them, which was a *damned* exciting idea. Tomorrow evening, hmm? "I can only guess at what brought this on," he said low and huskily. "But you won't be sorry, sweetheart."

Blair closed her eyes as a wave of heat engulfed her. Responding to Ace would never be a problem, obviously, but sexually inflaming dialogue wasn't her goal here.

"The invitation does not include me for dessert," she said bluntly.

Ace blinked. "Uh...sure, no problem. I'll behave, I promise."

"I'd appreciate it. See you tomorrow evening."

Ace put the phone down with a grimace. What the hell was going on now with Blair? He would better understand her call and dinner invitation if she had seen her doctor, but she hadn't and couldn't for another week.

Unless...

No, he thought. She wouldn't pull that kind of stunt.

Turning off the light, Ace stretched out and tried to get comfortable. But the idea, once born, wouldn't go away. If she had already seen her doctor and been diagnosed as pregnant, why wouldn't she admit it? And if for some peculiar reason she didn't want him knowing the truth, why make this overture? Why deliberately bring them together?

The concept of a child of his own did funny things to Ace. Never had he spent time fantasizing about a wife and children. He liked kids. Certainly he'd been close to his brother's two boys. He'd go back to Colorado and see them, of course. He and his brother weren't enemies, after all; they just couldn't run the same ranch.

Lying in the dark, Ace began to imagine a youngster on the place, a little boy or girl calling him daddy. Looking to him for guidance, for love. He'd put him or her on a horse very young. He'd...

He'd have a wife...Blair. She'd be in this bed with him every night. Ace rubbed his suddenly dry mouth as the image became painfully distinct. She was right about the two of them just barely knowing each other and marriage being a big step. But her raising their baby all by herself was a hell of a bigger step, and the possibility of her even contemplating doing it gave Ace a tremendous kick in his pride.

He'd told her this wasn't a kid's game, and it was getting more serious by the day. He liked women and there was a string of them in his past. But he meant what he'd said to Blair: no kid of his was going to be raised without his father.

The funny thing was, the idea of a permanent bond with Blair wasn't at all unappealing. Granted, it created some stress in his system. They had a lot to work through, but the feelings Blair had aroused right from the beginning had been more than the usual desire to bed a beautiful woman.

He would play the game by her rules, he decided. For a while, at least. Feel her out, see what she was up to. If his suspicions were wrong, no one would be hurt. But if they were right, Blair was going to have a fight on her hands. He wasn't going to stand by and do nothing while she went through pregnancy and childbirth all on her own, and that was final.

* * *

Blair opened the door to an unusually subdued guest the following evening. Ace thrust out a florist's bouquet of flowers, surprising her.

"Why... thank you," she stammered. His hair had been trimmed and was neatly brushed. He was wearing gray slacks, a light blue shirt and black loafers. Her heart was suddenly in her throat, because he had obviously gone to a lot of trouble for a simple supper invitation. "Come in."

"Thanks."

Inside, Blair brought him to the living room. "Go ahead and sit down. I'll put these in water." She sniffed one of the bud roses in the bouquet. "They're beautiful."

Internally edgy, Ace stood with his hands in his pants pockets while Blair went to the kitchen. He could hear her moving around, and his normal instinct urged him to go after her. She looked luscious in a pale pink sundress, kissable, lovable. If she was pregnant, nothing showed yet. But it probably wouldn't for weeks, maybe months. Hell, he didn't even know what to look for, other than a larger waistline.

She returned and placed the vase of flowers on the coffee table. "Please sit down," she told him before seating herself on the sofa.

Ace sank onto a chair, his gaze bold and steady. "You're pretty in pink."

She smiled. "Isn't that the name of a movie?"

"Is it?"

Blair waved away the topic. "You've probably been wondering why I asked you to dinner."

"It crossed my mind," Ace admitted dryly.

"Well, if there *is* a child," Blair said carefully, "its parents should at least be on speaking terms."

Doubts flickered through Ace. Maybe she hadn't seen her doctor. Maybe he'd jumped to the wrong conclusion last night.

"If there's a child," he said coolly, "its parents should be married."

Blair cleared her throat. "Not necessarily, Ace. People live differently today. Look at the Hollywood stars who prefer—"

Ace cut in. "Houghton, Montana, isn't Hollywood."

"Well, no, of course it isn't. But neither is it backwoods U.S.A. The people here are—"

"Like people in every other small town across the country. Don't think you wouldn't be judged, Blair, particularly if everyone knows your baby's father wants to marry you and you're refusing."

"You wouldn't spread it around!"

Ace looked away. "I don't know what I'd do, to tell you the truth." His eyes returned to her stricken face. "But I wouldn't be hiding out at my ranch and ignoring the whole thing, I can tell you that much." Looking at her, his attitude and voice softened. "Sugar, intentionally hurting you is the last thing I'd ever do."

The husky quality in his voice seemed to rip through Blair. He could turn her thoughts with a word, a gesture, from whatever topic, however serious, to sex. To that day in his bedroom. Since, as he'd promised, whenever her blood heated up, and it did heat, dammit, she thought of him. Being in the same room with him, in the same small house, and knowing that no one else was going to come along, was dynamite.

"Let me get you something to drink," she said with a tremulous smile, rising from the sofa. "What would you like?"

Wondering if she was going to run to another room every time he got too close to a personal topic, Ace said almost somberly, "What've you got?"

"Beer, soft drinks and iced tea."

"I'll have a beer, thanks."

Blair managed a dignified retreat. At least she hoped her fluster didn't show. In the privacy of the kitchen she stopped to lean her feverish forehead against the cool finish of the refrigerator door. Bandying words with Ace was a no-win proposition for her. All he had to do to undermine her composure was suggestively cock an eyebrow, or call her "sugar" in that bedroom voice of his.

His casual endearments had grated from the first, and now she knew why. Blair grabbed the refrigerator handle and yanked open the door. Noisily she removed a bottle of beer and the iced-tea pitcher.

In the living room Ace slowly stood up. Nonchalantly he strolled through the house to the kitchen doorway, where he lounged against the frame. "Something bothering you?"

Blair whirled. "You startled me!"

"Sorry."

Embarrassed because he'd heard her slamming things around, Blair got very busy finding glasses for the drinks. Dinner was in the oven, a simple casserole. The green salad was chilling in the fridge. The table was set. She felt Ace's gaze go from the oven to the table and back to her.

"Dinner will be ready in about fifteen minutes," she mumbled, turning her back on Ace to arrange the drinks and glasses on a tray.

When she started to pick up the tray, however, Ace came closer. "Let me take that."

"Thank you." Without looking at him, Blair left the tray on the counter and stalked to the living room and sat down.

Ace did the serving, lowering the tray so she could take her glass of iced tea. Smiling as though nothing was amiss, he set the tray on the coffee table, unscrewed the top on the beer bottle and resumed his chair, leaving the glass behind.

Blair took a healthy swallow of her tea. "Well," she said while her mind raced for a neutral topic. "How're things going with the ranch?"

"Good," Ace replied. "Real good. How are things going at the bank?"

"Good. Uh ... fine. Busy, as usual."

They drank some more and then looked at each other. Ace grinned. "Guess we'll never win any prizes in the small-talk department."

"How...how did you happen to choose Montana?" Blair blurted.

Ace sat back. "I was through this area a few years ago. Me and Virge. Just nosing around, you know? Anyway, when Dave and I made the deal on the home ranch, I remembered Houghton. The Sutter place was within my financial reach, where most of the other spreads for sale weren't. That helped make up my mind. Do you like to ride?"

"Ride?"

"Horses. Are you a rider?"

She gave her head a shake. "Never had much opportunity. Oh, a few times I visited one friend or another who had horses and we did some riding, but that's about it."

"We'll have to see to your education, honey," Ace said softly. "Later, though, when we know for sure if you're pregnant or not. Probably wouldn't be a good idea to take it up now."

It wouldn't be. Dr. Miller had told her to keep on doing whatever was customary, along with long walks, but not to develop a sudden fancy for bowling or tennis, for example, if those were new activities. *Just use common sense, avoid alcohol and tobacco, eat right and take those walks, and you'll increase your odds of delivering a healthy baby, Blair.*

But the thought of Ace teaching her to ride a horse was surprisingly pleasant. Unable to look directly at him at this moment, Blair murmured, "Well, we'll see."

Over the bottle of beer while taking a swallow, Ace eyed her evasive expression and was stunned to experience what felt like a revelation. She *was* pregnant, and this invitation was a fishing expedition. She was testing him, trying to decide if he was good enough to take their relationship into the future.

He didn't know whether to be angry or elated. She wasn't going to admit anything to him and would probably lie through her pretty teeth if he pressed for honesty. So, what was her game plan, to wait until she was showing and *then* make up her mind about the future? His patience was sorely tried by Blair's attitude, stretched thin enough that he considered walking out of there and never coming back. Few people had ever gotten away with telling Ace Barclay when to jump and how high, and Blair doing it under these circumstances grated on raw nerves.

He tipped the beer bottle and nearly finished it. Then his gaze became sardonic. "How come you're drinking tea? Don't you like beer?"

"I like beer once in a while. Tonight I feel like tea. Is that a problem for you?" She leaned forward suddenly. "Let's clarify something, Ace. What you drink, eat, don't drink, don't eat, enjoy doing in your free time, *hate* doing in your free time, are some of your rights as a free and responsible individual. You don't have to explain your preferences to anyone, nor do you have to apologize if they happen to differ from your companion's. I claim the same rights."

Ace couldn't hold back a snort of laughter. "All of that because I asked if you like beer? What got you on that soapbox?"

"Am I wrong? Do you disagree with anything I said?"

"Does it matter what I think? Apparently you're one of those liberated women who live in dread of someone—a man, especially—stepping on their rights."

"Have you known enough 'liberated' women to make you an expert on the subject?"

Her sarcastic tone annoyed Ace. "It's not a subject I've even thought of before, but if you want my honest opinion, it's hogwash in an important relationship."

Blair coolly raised an eyebrow. "Is that a fact? How enlightening. My mother was a very wise woman, and she viewed 'rights' for both men and women as highly crucial to a successful relationship. Surely you don't believe in the old fairy tale about a married couple living happily ever after simply because they've sworn to love and honor each other for the rest of their lives, do you?''

`"Fairy tales are for kids, but don't try to convince me that any two people can make a go of it without bending to each other's likes and dislikes. I think it's called adjustment,'' Ace drawled before draining the beer bottle.

"And what about respect?''

"Respect for what?''

"For each other's point of view. Do you know of any two people who think exactly alike on every topic?''

"Hell, no,'' Ace admitted. He held up the empty bottle. "Got another one of these?''

Blair left her place on the sofa to get him another beer, which she promptly carried to the living room and placed in his hand. "Then what do you think those two people should do when they find themselves facing an impasse? Suppose he feels one way about something and she feels differently. Who's right? Who's wrong?''

Ace rubbed his chin with his fingertips. "What the hell brought on this conversation? Look, I don't know any more about how we'd get along if we were married than you do, but...''

"I was *not* talking about you and me!'' Blair broke in heatedly. "Why did you assume I was? This is a perfect example of how two people can misinterpret each other's remarks.''

He looked at her for the longest time, then said, "I suppose you were talking about the couple next door, right? Or one in the next block? Blair, I'll discuss any subject you want to name, but don't try to con me.''

"Conning'' him was precisely what she was doing, but not so much as an eyelash flickered on her face. She refused to allow guilt to interfere with her plan. Ace wasn't going to slither into her and the baby's life on sex appeal alone, no man was. Her subservient relationship with Derek was her own fault. Its demise was inevitable as she would not have remained a mere accessory to Derek's decisions for long. But she had learned from that mistake and would not repeat it.

At the sound of the oven timer buzzing in the kitchen, Blair stood up. "Dinner is ready."

Ace wondered when he could make a polite exit. Throughout the surprisingly tasty meal and over coffee in the living room afterward, they had both avoided controversial subjects so diligently that the evening had become bland enough to be boring.

It hadn't had to be. There were enough unacknowledged sparks between him and Blair to light up a dark night, but her unrelenting reserve stated unequivocally, "Hands off!" Ace was tiring of the game, and the idea of pinning her down with a roster of straightforward questions was becoming difficult to contain. But deciding that pressure at this point would do more harm than good, he stood up and lazily stretched his back. "I think it's time to go. Thanks for having me over. You're a good cook."

His stretch struck Blair as the most erotic movement she'd ever seen a man make. On second thought, nearly every movement Ace made had erotic tendencies. Did he know how sexy his smile was? Undoubtedly, she thought with some self-disgust at the inanity of that question. As cocky as he was, he probably wallowed in conceit over his looks.

She got up and preceded him to the front door. "Thank you for coming."

Ace was right behind her, but he gave her room to open the door, standing then with his hand on it. "Do we kiss good-night, or what?"

Blair's eyes slid away from his. "I opt for the 'or what,' Ace. Let's just..."

Swiftly his free hand rose to cup the back of her head. His mouth covered hers in a hard, possessive kiss that lasted longer than he had intended, long enough that he felt the quivering response of her lips and the quickened rate of his own pulse. But he'd done enough ineffectual begging with Blair.

"G'night, babe," he whispered huskily. "See you around."

Teetering on legs that had become dangerously rubbery, Blair watched him skip off of her front stoop and down the sidewalk to his pickup at the curb. He hadn't asked for another date. He hadn't suggested that either of them call the other. Instead he had kissed her as though he owned her and left her feeling dazed from the impact.

"You...you *gunslinger*," she whispered raggedly, emphasizing the insulting term. Slamming the door shut and hoping he grasped her anger in the bang, she immediately switched off the porch light and hoped he would see the hasty gesture as rude. He was the most infuriating, annoying, irritating person she'd ever known!

But what bothered her most about the evening was that she had hardly been able to choke down any dinner, which was much too reminiscent of her mother's story about falling in love with Blair's father.

Falling in love with Ace—especially now—would completely disarm her. Losing detachment and an ability to reason at this point of her life would destroy every chance she had of making a sensible decision about the future.

She couldn't let it happen, she just couldn't!

Nine

In the next few days Blair's moods swung from cringing cowardice to enough bravery to merit a medal. She could do it alone, she told herself with profound confidence one moment, and the next she would be mentally cowering over what could only be a bleak and hapless future.

Her options were neither plentiful nor appealing: she could leave Houghton and go somewhere completely new or to Mitch, she could brazen it out right where she was, or she could accept Ace's offer of marriage.

He called every evening. "How're you doing?"

"I'm doing fine." It wasn't quite a lie, though neither was it quite the truth. In many ways she was functioning as usual; it wasn't the present disturbing her nearly as much as the unknown future.

He invited her to the ranch. "I'm planning on getting started with some renovations in the house, and I'd like to hear your ideas."

"Ace, I'm not a decorator."

"Maybe not, but women seem to have an instinct about colors and things."

"I don't." *That* was a lie. Not only did she possess a fine instinct for coordinating "colors and things," she enjoyed doing it. Her own house was neither spacious nor fancy, but it was nicely decorated.

On the third night after their dinner together, Ace became more insistent. "We have to see each other."

Blair wasn't so certain; their last meeting had been an awful flop, in her estimation. "Maybe later on."

"How much later?"

"I don't know. Don't push me, Ace."

"How long are you going to keep this up?"

She didn't pretend to misunderstand. "I don't know."

Ace said a terse good-night and put down the phone. Enough was enough. Blair's unfairness was making him impatient with everyone around him. Poor ol' Virge was bearing the brunt of Ace's jagged emotions and today had barked back. A breach with his oldest and best friend was one side effect of this mess with Blair that he wasn't going to tolerate.

After stewing about it for over an hour, Ace tore through the house and out the back door. Jumping into his pickup, he started the engine and drove away fast enough that the tires kicked up gravel. Fifteen minutes later he pulled into Blair's driveway. Slamming the truck's door behind him, he strode to Blair's front door and knocked.

The house was silent and remained dark. He knocked again, louder. The door opened a crack. "Ace! I was in bed!"

"I want to come in."

"Not tonight."

"Yes, tonight!" Ace pushed the door open.

Blair had no choice but to step back out of his way. "You have no right to come barging in here like this!" Her nightgown was short and flimsy, and though there weren't any lights burning, she felt exposed.

"Don't start talking about rights again," Ace muttered. "I want some plain conversation, and I'm not leaving till I get it." He tapped Blair on the chest, a gesture she shied from. Barely noticing, Ace kept on talking. "Did you see your doctor or didn't you? And if not, why not? And don't hand me any more of that crap about him being out of touch. I wasn't born yesterday, nor am I dense."

Blair whirled completely away from him and his blustery anger. "No, but you're damned pushy!"

He followed her into the dark living room. "Stop with the games, Blair. I want a straight answer. Are you pregnant?" He was aware of her sinking to the sofa. Her long silence was all the answer he needed. Silent himself, he fell back onto a chair. After a minute he released the breath he'd been holding. "So what do you want to do?"

Blair spoke in a low voice. "That's what I've been trying to figure out."

"You're looking for a solution that excludes me, aren't you?" He sounded accusing.

"Since you're demanding the truth, yes."

"Why?"

Her tone became scathingly derogatory. "Need you ask?"

"You don't hate me, so don't try to convince me you do."

"What an ego you have," she drawled. "It must be nice to be so sure of yourself."

"Sure of myself! With you? Now, there's a laugh."

"Laugh all you want. I'm going back to bed. Make sure the door is locked when you leave." Getting up, Blair started from the living room.

But she had to pass Ace's chair and the darkness obscured his quick reflexes. One second she was on her feet and moving, and the next she was in a heap on his lap. Stunned, she felt his arms clamp around her.

He spoke deep in his throat. "Don't struggle. It won't do you any good."

"Now you're resorting to force?" The sarcasm she'd attempted sounded more like a caress, startling her. "Let me go, Ace.'' Her voice became a husky whisper. ''Please let me go.''

''Not yet.'' He moved his face against her hair, inhaling its scent, absorbing its texture. Blair on his lap in the dark was what he'd been yearning for, aching for. Their one time together was a haunting memory, a *taunting* memory. How many times since had he awakened in the night to remember it, to sweat over it?

He could feel her tension, and how she was trying to maintain an impossible distance. ''Relax,'' he whispered. ''You feel good. So good.''

But Blair knew what would happen if she relaxed an iota. The hard fast beat of her own heart felt choking. Her throat was tight, her mouth dry. He was doing nothing but holding her in place, but his size and maleness seemed to be surrounding her. His body was both hard and yielding, a mystery. His clothing felt soft and smelled clean. Her head started swimming.

''You have to let me go,'' she said hoarsely.

''I don't *have* to do anything.'' He began nuzzling her throat.

''Don't, Ace. This isn't the answer.''

''Maybe it is,'' he whispered. ''Maybe it's the answer to everything.'' His lips slowly moved upward to her face.

She tipped her head, and his mouth touched only the corner of hers. ''I'm not going to...to...'' Her protest evolved into a sensual sigh. As had happened in his bedroom that day, his sexuality was overwhelming her.

Holding her head in the crook of his arm, he began feathering kisses to her face. Blair's limbs were suddenly weak and heavy. ''You're not a very nice person,'' she groaned.

''A gunslinger, I believe you called me before.''

''It's hardly a label to gloat over.''

''Am I gloating?'' Ace wasn't breathing easily. He hadn't come to Blair's with this in mind. Grabbing her had been strictly an impulse. Holding her on his lap against her will might not be completely aboveboard, but how else was he ever going to get through to her?

On the other hand, this could be going too far. Blair had mentioned force, and he'd never forced a woman into anything in his life. At precisely the same moment that he finally managed to land a solid kiss to her mouth he relaxed his arms, giving her all the freedom she needed to break away.

She didn't break away. She lay on his lap, warm and sweet and sexy in her silky, skimpy gown, and kissed him back with as much passion as he was kissing her. He forgot everything else and slid his tongue into her willing mouth, while his eager hand began roaming the exciting contours of her waist and breasts. The fabric of her gown was slippery to the touch. The darkness and Blair's response ignited Ace's imagination. Locating the hem of her short gown, he glided his hand up her thigh.

Then he nearly lost it: she wasn't wearing panties!

"Blair...baby..." His voice was so thick he barely recognized it. His kiss became hungry.

Her sigh was one of resignation. And desire. Desire for this rough-hewn, insolent, pushy man, who had disrupted her life and stolen her virginity.

No, he hadn't stolen anything. She'd given willingly, and why wouldn't he or any other man take what had been offered so fervently?

She snuggled closer to his chest, kissed him back and allowed him to explore under her gown. His touch was gentle but certain. Along with her own pleasure Blair was aware of Ace's. The anger he'd arrived with had vanished, apparently, and what had happened to her own?

In this they connected. In caresses and kisses and embraces, they were so in tune she couldn't withhold it from him or herself. He knew her secret now, and was he more tender because of it? Did he feel something special because she was carrying his child? If he attempted to talk about feelings, would she listen?

Blair's questions disappeared within the maelstrom of sensations Ace was arousing. Accepting her own sensuality was an enormous step for her, but finding herself in Ace's arms again and loving his power over her senses made denial impossible. His tongue in her mouth felt heavenly; his hand between her legs felt sinfully delicious. There was only one conclusion to so much need, and she was beyond resisting its lure.

Breathing huskily, she moved her lips from his mouth to his ear to whisper, "Would you like to see my bedroom?"

His reply was a heaving up out of the chair, lifting her along with himself. "Which way?" he mumbled thickly. The darkness of Blair's house was confusing.

"Straight ahead and to the left." She laughed softly, throatily. Being carried to bed was an excitement she had only read about, and it was exciting, incredibly so, making her tingly and feverish.

"This door," she directed after a minute.

Ace stopped at the doorway. "Turn on a light, Blair."

"But I like the dark," she whispered.

He hesitated—his preference was to see her—but he didn't want her suddenly changing her mind. Not now. Not when he was burning with inner fires. He hadn't come here to seduce Blair, but things seemed to happen between them without plan or direction.

He entered the dark bedroom, sensing more than seeing the bulk of the bed. Nearing it, he let her feet slide to the floor. She melted against him, feeling soft and womanly. Groaning, he squeezed her closer and kissed her passionately, lifting her gown to roam her bare back and hips. "If I'm a gunslinger, you're a siren," he whispered raggedly.

The comment made Blair smile. Her, a siren? Blair Conover, loan officer? Her smile faded. This loan officer was going to shock the good citizens of Houghton. Maybe this loan officer wouldn't *be* a loan officer after that. Could the bank discharge an employee on the basis of moral laxity?

There were laws against that sort of discrimination, weren't there?

Still, would she have the nerve to fight a decision of that nature? Air her personal linen in such a public way?

She shivered from her thoughts. "You're getting cold," Ace whispered, urging her to the bed and under the covers. Undressing quickly, practically tearing off his clothes in his haste, he joined her in bed.

His hot skin against hers gave Blair another shiver, but it was the most pleasurable of sensations and she whispered, "I'm not shivering because I'm cold. It's your doing."

"I make you shivery?" Ace chuckled softly. "You make me so hot I could melt an iceberg."

"That, too," Blair murmured only a heartbeat before he claimed her lips. Somehow, within the kiss, her nightgown vanished. Aware only of sensual movement, Ace's body against hers, his mouth on hers, the subtle sliding of fabric was barely noticed.

Admittedly Blair's mind was spinning. She wanted Ace's arms around her and felt that she could contentedly lie there and savor his taste and scent for the rest of her days. Still, behind her euphoria was unease and a vague recognition that life did not consist solely of pleasure. She would, she knew, regret this later.

"I'm going to make love to you all night," Ace whispered huskily.

All thoughts of regret dissolved into nothingness for Blair. Ace's declaration could only be a macho boast, but it brought the tenor of their embrace to a fever pitch. Seductively she whispered, "I'm with you."

Three seconds later he was on top of her, thrusting into her, growling his pleasure, and she *was* with him, whimpering, clinging, lifting her hips to match his rhythm. Vague thoughts leapt through her feverish brain. Maybe she'd always known this would happen again. Maybe she'd even been hoping it would. Ace had said it would, and Ace was far more experienced than she would ever be.

The idea of Ace's "experience" was surprisingly discomfiting. Blair closed her mind to it. It was obvious that Ace wasn't thinking of any other woman right now, and her doing so was ludicrous.

"You're perfect," he mumbled thickly. "Perfect."

So was he, though his wildly passionate kiss prevented Blair from saying so. Her skin was damp; so was his. Her breathing was raspy and erratic; so was his. He slid his hands beneath her hips to lift her higher; she wrapped her legs around him. The bedclothes slithered to the floor; neither noticed. He stopped moving to kiss her breasts; she moaned deep in her throat and held his head to keep his mouth where it was.

She was suddenly at the peak. Tears began seeping from her eyes. "Ace...Ace..." It was a cry from her soul, a plea.

He heard it and understood. Everything else faded in their final rush to fulfillment.

Dazed by the strength of her own pleasure, Blair found speech impossible for several minutes. She lay there stunned, thinking about it while Ace cooled down. Was flawless sexuality enough for a couple? This was what had been missing from her and Derek's relationship, and it had to be a crucial component in a good marriage. But was it enough?

Ace raised his head and tried to focus on Blair's face in the dark. "Damn, you're something," he whispered. "I might never get enough of you, sweetheart."

"In bed."

"You got that right." Ace aimed for her lips and was surprised when she turned her head. "Did I do something wrong?"

"I'm sure you're the best," Blair said, her voice husky from the tears in her throat. "I'm also sure that you know it."

Ace's eyes squinted. "I did do something wrong. Are you mad because I pulled you down on my lap?"

"I'm not mad at anything. Please let me up."

He didn't move. "If you're not mad, what are you? You liked it, didn't you? I was sure you were with me. You said you were."

"Ace, I don't want to have this conversation. Please let me up."

Reluctantly Ace moved on the bed. Immediately Blair got up and left the room. He could see her only as a pale form in the inky blackness, and straining his eyes to see in the dark was beginning to grate on his nerves, right along with Blair's ongoing attitude. Obviously she wasn't happy with the aftermath of their making love again, and why in hell not?

Feeling around for the switch on the bedside lamp, he turned it on then blinked at the sudden infusion of light. Other than the sheet under him, the bed was completely devoid of blankets. Peering over the edge and spotting the bedding, he hauled it up and over himself.

Then he lay there and waited for Blair to come back.

She took her time in the bathroom, not at all anxious to return to Ace. A forced marriage couldn't possibly turn out well, and picturing herself trapped in a situation with a resentful man was a painful exercise. Other than that overwhelming sexuality between them, she sensed very little from Ace in the way of feelings. He enjoyed sex with her, and obviously she lost every vestige of will and reason when he turned on the charm, but what about love?

Blair frowned at herself in the mirror. Love was a mystical emotion, and did she fully understand her own expectations with regard to the term? Maybe she expected too much. When had her ground rules for marriage become so idealistic? She had, after all, been happily contemplating marriage with Derek, and there had been numerous imperfections marring their relationship. Why did she demand so much from Ace? Obviously he was giving her what he could, what he had to give. Why wasn't it enough?

Her idealism was going to cause an enormous amount of trouble, for herself, for her child, and yes, probably for Ace.

Looking at her situation realistically, wasn't she beyond holding out for perfection?

Sighing, Blair took the robe from the hook on the bathroom door and put it on. She had made her bed and must lie in it. There was no one to blame for her predicament but herself, and longing for Utopia when she had Houghton, Montana, to deal with was adolescent foolishness.

Snapping off the bathroom light and opening the door, Blair was stopped, briefly, by the light coming from the bedroom. Gathering her courage, she walked in. Ace looked dug in and comfortable in her bed, though his expression was a little wary.

His gaze flicked over her robe. "Feeling any better?"

"I'm feeling—" Blair paused "—brutally vulnerable."

"What d'you mean by that?"

Lingering near the bureau, Blair absently picked up a bottle of cologne and after a moment set it down again. "Is that proposal of marriage still open?"

Ace hoisted himself to an elbow. "Would I be here if it wasn't?"

"Do I know you well enough to analyze your actions?"

His eyes narrowed. "You're thinking of us getting married, but you're not happy about it."

"I doubt if the prospect of a shotgun marriage ever made anyone happy. You're going to end up resenting it, you know. And resenting me, as well. It won't be a good marriage, and it probably won't last."

Ace's face hardened. "My brother's wife was pregnant when they got married, and they have a damned good marriage. You're looking for problems, Blair. Deliberately. We might..."

She held up a hand, breaking in. "I don't expect moonlight and roses, Ace, and I would appreciate a frank discussion without a lot of silly notions."

"Silly notions," he repeated darkly. "Like what?" He threw back the blankets and got off the bed, completely ignoring his nudity.

But Blair couldn't ignore it. Flushing hotly, she turned away. "Please get dressed."

Sudden fury rocketed through Ace. "If you're thinking of separate beds after the wedding, then you're right about 'silly notions'!" He took Blair's arm and turned her around to glare into her eyes. "We'll share the same bed, sugar, bet on it."

His drawling sarcasm and the insulting way he'd said "sugar" felt like staccato blows to Blair's nervous system. Before she could vocalize her sudden outrage, however, Ace went on. "You know what you are, Blair, baby? A hypocrite. Not ten minutes ago you were under me on that bed and loving it. Now you're embarrassed because I'm naked? Grow up, sugar. After we're married, you're going to see me naked a lot."

"I wouldn't marry you if you were the last man on earth!" she shrieked, giving her arm a sharp shake to break his grasp. "In the first damned place I wasn't talking about separate beds, though that's the only good idea I've ever heard come out of your mouth!"

Ace's lip curled. "Then what were you talking about?"

"About a normal marriage. About impossible expectations. About affection, and permanence, and..." She threw up her hands. "Just forget it. We will never communicate beyond..."

Ace finished the sentence for her, turning it into a question. "Beyond sex? That's your concept of our relationship, babe, not mine."

"Stop calling me those insufferable names!"

"Then stop behaving like a petulant child!" Ace moved closer to her. "Blair, we made a baby. All right, it shocked us both. But we're going to be parents. I'm ready to accept the responsibility. Don't you think it's time you did?"

Her eyes shot lethal sparks. "You...you...*jerk!* How dare you suggest I'm irresponsible! I'm trying to do what's best for everyone concerned. Even for you!"

That caused a lull, during which Ace untangled his briefs and jeans and put on the underwear. Blair didn't watch. Instead she restlessly moved around the room. Their passionate outburst was cowing. Obviously Ace wasn't a man to be led by the nose, which she remembered figuring out during their first meeting. Their second, actually, the day he brought Virge to her house.

"Let's talk without yelling, okay?" Ace said.

Blair turned to face him. "It's what I suggested before, if you care to remember. A frank discussion."

"Without silly notions," Ace reminded with a faint grimace. "Look, the only reason our marriage wouldn't work is if we didn't *want* it to work. I'm sure willing to give it every effort."

Blair became very still. "Do you really want the baby?"

Ace hesitated. "Blair...I don't know what I want. The idea of a baby is...." He looked at her. "Help me out here. Aren't you stunned by the idea of a baby?"

"It's not merely an idea. It's a fact," Blair stated coolly.

"It was only a suspicion to me until about an hour ago," Ace said while raking his hair in an agitated gesture. He dropped his hand. "Yes, I want the baby."

"Your enthusiasm is enormously comforting."

"What the hell do you want me to say, that I'm thrilled? Maybe I'll be thrilled tomorrow. Give me a little time to get used to it, Blair." Looking at her, he sensed her misery. She looked small and forlorn, and her prideful expression could only be bravado.

He took the few steps between them and put his hands on her shoulders. "Let's not fight anymore." His voice was low and compelling. "Fighting isn't what I want to do with you, Blair."

She knew what he wanted to do with her. What hurt so much was that she wanted the same thing with him. However far apart they were on the realities of their relationship, they functioned as one entity in the bedroom. No, they wouldn't be using separate beds during their marriage, but she still had no faith in its longevity.

"No more tonight," she said huskily, and took a backward step. "I'd like you to leave now."

Ace's eyes searched hers. "Did we settle anything?"

Blair gave a nod. "Yes, but you mentioned needing some time and so do I. I never used my vacation from the bank this summer. I'd like to do so."

"Would you go somewhere?"

"I might visit my brother in Seattle." She looked away. "I don't know. Nothing's definite."

"You just now thought of it, didn't you?"

She was beyond pretense. "Yes."

Ace was thinking. "Maybe it would be a good idea if we went somewhere together."

"No. I want to be alone." Ducking away from him, Blair moved to the other side of the room. "When I get back we can decided on a . . . on the . . ."

"Wedding date?" Ace snagged his jeans from the floor and began shoving his feet into them. "Why is that so tough for you to say?" He zipped his fly.

"It's tough for you to say, too, so please don't patronize me." The rasp of his zipper had unnerved Blair. Watching him dress was almost as intimate as watching him undress. He was a fever in her blood, and she wished ardently that he wasn't.

Ace stood there buttoning his shirt. "You must think that getting away by yourself is going to help."

"It couldn't hurt. I need to do some thinking."

"But we're definitely going to be married when you get back." Ace tucked the tails of his shirt into his jeans.

"I guess we are." Blair sighed.

He looked at her. "You're not thrilled, either."

"No, I'm not thrilled." But she *was* heartbroken, and positive that she would shed buckets of tears after he'd gone. This had to be the most dismal conversation any two people had ever devised on the subject of marriage. Their decision was sensible from Blair's point of view, and for the baby's, as well. Ace was doing the honorable thing, offering his hand and his name. What more could she hope for? They weren't in love, after all.

Ace sat on the bed to put on his socks. He lifted his eyes to Blair and experienced a jolting tenderness. "Come over here, honey."

To the bed? Blair shook her head.

He patted the bed. "Just to sit by me. I promise."

Was this a bid for warmth from Ace? For something other than sexual communion? Blair hesitated. They were going to be married, and refusing any possibility of warmth between them could be a dire mistake.

Still, she didn't rush to the bed. When she reached it Ace took her hand and drew her down to sit next to him. He wound their fingers together. "Blair, we're in this together. Whatever else you think of while you're gone, remember that, will you?"

Tears filled her eyes. "I will."

"And don't cry, honey." He brought her head to his chest. "Please don't cry. Everything will be fine, you'll see." He rubbed her back, gently, slowly. And then he gritted his teeth, because the inevitable was happening in his jeans. "Damn, you affect me," he whispered hoarsely. "Your hormones, or something, make mine go crazy."

Blair's tears flowed harder. "You make me a little crazy, too."

"But that's not anything to cry about." Closing his eyes, Ace moved his mouth in her hair, which had just about the most arousing scent he'd ever smelled. "Is it?" he whispered.

"Then why am I crying?"

"Because you want me again and you wish you didn't? Blair, our marriage might not be moonbeams and roses, as you said, but it sure as hell won't be dull." He lay back and pulled Blair with him.

"You promised . . ."

"And I meant it." Cupping the back of her head with his hand, he brought her mouth down to his. The kiss was wet and sexy and rife with feelings that set Blair's mind to spinning. Was something going on between her and Ace that neither had put into words or even thoughts? Or was this crazy, sudden sensation of belonging to Ace completely one-sided? What if she were the only one feeling so torn up?

Indeed, she did need to get away by herself. And she would, just as soon as she could speak to Mr. Hendrix about taking her vacation time now. *Now!* Not a month down the road.

With Ace's hands occupied elsewhere, primarily on her backside, Blair broke the kiss and raised her head to see his eyes. Tenderness was in her system and with the slightest encouragement from him it would be very easy to let it show.

But, sadly, all she saw in Ace's dark blue eyes was the glaze of renewing desire. Firmly Blair disengaged herself from his embrace and got off the bed. He sat up, startled.

"Good night," she said quietly.

"You want me to leave." Slowly Ace pulled himself up to his feet.

"I want you to leave," she confirmed, edging toward the bedroom doorway.

Ace followed. "May I call you tomorrow?"

"Call if you wish."

Snapping on lights as they went, Blair escorted him to the front door. His truck had been parked in her driveway for some time, and the neighbors could have noticed. Blair sighed and opened the door.

"Good night, Ace."

He paused before her. "You won't leave town without telling me, will you?"

"No."

After a moment he nodded. "All right. I'll talk to you tomorrow." Bending quickly, he planted a kiss on her lips. "G'night, sugar."

She had already told him good-night twice, but she murmured the words again, then closed the door behind him.

Turning out the lights again, she returned to her bedroom, straightened the sheets and blankets on the bed, donned a fresh nightgown and lay down.

But her eyes were wide open and staring, and she didn't count on falling immediately asleep.

Which was just as well, as sleep eluded her for hours.

Ten

Blair spoke to the bank manager at the first available opportunity the next morning. Mr. Hendrix had no objection to her using her vacation time right away, providing her pending loans could be handled by Winona.

"I'll speak to Winona about it, of course," Blair said. "But I'm sure she will agree. We always take care of each other's work during any absences."

Winona readily agreed to tending Blair's clients, and, in fact, told Blair she was glad to see her planning to take some time off. "You've been looking a little peaked, Blair. Are you feeling all right?"

It was the first time anyone had hinted that all might not be a hundred percent with Blair's health. As innocuous as Winona's concern was, it hit home for Blair. Right now the changes in her body were subtle and barely discernible; in a very short time her condition would become glaringly obvious. She had to make up her mind about marrying Ace, or else better prepare herself for the future without him.

Mr. Hendrix's permission and Winona's cooperation resulted in Blair's next task: deciding what to do with her two weeks away from the bank. She would love to visit Mitch, but bringing her unsolved dilemma to Seattle seemed grossly unfair to her brother. He was doing well in his job, but during past conversations he had talked about working long hours and squeezing in classes to learn about business procedures in the free time that he did have. Blair was proud that he seemed so determined to better himself, and she figured that the last thing Mitch needed was for her to descend with a sad story.

So...Seattle was out. Mitch would spot something wrong at first sight of her, and as sure as grass was green she would blurt out her tale of woe. He had accepted the demise of her wedding plans as she had expected, with complete understanding and predictions of better things to come. She would leave it at that for now.

Intermittently throughout the morning the subject arose in Blair's mind. Where would she go for two weeks? Depleting her savings account on an extravagant vacation wouldn't be at all wise right now, but neither did she want to merely hole up in her house and worry. A change of scene might clear her mind of normal everyday clutter and bring about a little decisiveness, but which change of scene? A cabin in the mountains? A resort near a body of water? Someplace that was busy and active, or a quiet retreat?

She had a little time to decide. Today was Thursday, which meant one more working day before the weekend.

During her lunch break Blair went to Houghton's one travel agency and picked up a handful of brochures for Montana-based resorts. She knew the lady on duty, Martha Wicks.

"Planning a vacation?" Martha asked cheerfully.

"On rather short notice, I'm afraid," Blair murmured while thumbing through the glossy brochures. She looked up at Martha. "Will that be a problem?"

"How soon are you talking about?"

"This coming Saturday."

Martha shook her head. "I don't know, Blair. All we can do is call the places that interest you and ask if anything's available."

"I'll look these over and phone you later."

"Fine."

A few minutes later at the drive-in, sitting in her car with a sandwich and a carton of milk, Blair looked through the brochures. Choosing two as possibilities, she drove back to the bank and called Martha.

"I'll check with them immediately and call you right back," Martha promised.

Twenty minutes later Martha relayed disappointing news. "I'm sorry, Blair, but both places are booked solid for weeks. I'm afraid we would hear the same thing no matter who we called on such short notice."

Two hours later Martha called again. "Blair, I found something you might like. It's not a resort, but it's a very pleasant place. Rather isolated, however, so if that's a problem..."

"What is it, Martha?"

"A quite modern log cabin on a small fishing lake about a hundred miles from here. The owner occasionally rents it out, very selectively, I might add. I assured him of your good care, but I made it clear that I hadn't yet spoken to you about it. What do you think? Are you interested?"

"What would it cost, Martha?"

"Two hundred a week. It's fully furnished right down to bedding and towels, and the kitchen is completely equipped. All you'd have to take with you is food. I've seen the place myself, Blair. The owner is a friend of my husband's, and we spent a weekend out there last summer. The lake is lovely, very small and private. The only drawback for a woman alone is its isolation. It doesn't have a telephone and you wouldn't see another living soul during your stay."

"How are the roads?"

"Oh, the roads are fine. If I recall correctly, there are about twenty miles of gravel road just prior to reaching the site, but we drove our family car and didn't have any trouble."

"It sounds...nice." Blair was thinking hard. Was not seeing another living soul for two weeks a drawback for her? Wasn't that what she needed, utter peace and quiet in which to do her thinking? "Martha, I'll take it. Do I stop by and give you a check, or what?"

"Bring it by tomorrow, Blair. I'll have the keys to the cabin and a map all ready for you."

"Great. See you then. And thanks, Martha. I really appreciate your time on this."

The more Blair thought of that isolated cabin, the more satisfied she became with her decision to take it. That evening she began choosing and laying out casual clothing for the two weeks. After work tomorrow she would shop for food. She would leave early on Saturday morning. It felt good to have a definite plan in mind, and she realized that was precisely the goal she must strive for in her decision about Ace.

But she didn't want to think about Ace now. After she had arrived at the cabin and gotten settled was soon enough to begin seriously sifting through her own emotions and doubts where Ace was concerned. Her reluctance with Ace vaguely touched on Derek, for some odd reason, which needed looking into. Not that Ace wasn't every bit as reluctant as she was. Last night he'd admitted he wasn't thrilled about the baby, and what else could she conclude but that neither would he be thrilled if she agreed to marry him?

Sighing, then checking the light outside through her bedroom window, Blair decided it wasn't too late to wash her car. Even though she would be driving some gravel roads on Saturday, she preferred starting out in a clean car.

Quickly she changed into a pair of old cutoff jeans and a T-shirt. With a bucket of soapy water, a sponge, some towels and the garden hose handy, she backed her car out of the garage and parked it in the driveway. The front half of the car had been washed and she was soaping down the trunk and back end when Ace's pickup pulled up at the curb.

To Blair's dismay her heart skipped a beat. Frowning over the unexpected reaction, she straightened from her work and waited for Ace to get out and walk over to her. "I thought you were only going to call this evening."

"Decided this would be better." Ace's gaze boldly caressed the curves of her body in that T-shirt. Blair not only saw him doing it, she *felt* him doing it. There were moments when she forgot about his gunslinger tendencies, but a look like that was a definitive reminder.

"Do you undress every woman you meet with your eyes, or am I a special case?" she asked tensely, suddenly hot under the collar.

Startled, Ace backed up a step. "Hey, I didn't come here to get into another fight with you."

Her lips pursing, Blair turned back to the car and began scrubbing it furiously. "Leave me alone, Ace. There are times when you just naturally rub me the wrong way."

"Obviously," he drawled with heavy sarcasm, which earned him another dirty look from Blair. "Cool down, sugar. I only stopped by to find out about that vacation you mentioned last night. Did you make any definite plans yet?"

"I'm leaving on Saturday morning," Blair said stiffly.

This Saturday morning? How long would she be gone? Where was she going? It was difficult to ask questions when she seemed ardently intent on scrubbing the paint off the car! "Stand still for a few minutes, will you?"

"I want to get this done before dark." Blair bent over for the garden hose. "Get back if you don't want to get wet," she warned.

Ace moved out of the way and waited while she rinsed away the soap. When she began drying the car with towels, he hastened to help. They worked in silence. Blair had no choice but to thank him when the car was finished, but her voice wasn't exactly laden with enthusiasm. Still silent, she returned the car to the garage, then got out to put away the bucket and other cleaning gear.

Throughout, Ace was trying to maintain some patience. Finally everything was put away. It was getting dark. "Can I come in?" he asked.

The prospect of a repeat of last night's misstep in her own bed was unnerving. Ace himself was unnerving. His jeans fit his lean body too well and so did his shirt. His hair was mussed just enough, appearing as devilishly sexy. If she wasn't going to marry him, she had to stop making love with him!

"Uh...not tonight. Come around back. We can sit on the patio."

Ace followed her around the house. When she sat, he sat. Then he looked at her, long and hard. Blair squirmed. "You were asking about my vacation. As I said, I'm leaving on Saturday morning. I'll be gone for two weeks."

"Two weeks! Why so long?"

"Two weeks isn't long."

"It's *damned* long. What do you expect me to do while you're gone, twiddle my thumbs and worry about whether I'm good enough for you to marry?"

Blair flushed. "That's a rude thing to say."

"But it's the truth, isn't it?"

"I have never thought myself better than you or anyone else, so no, it is not the truth. But I nearly made one very bad mistake with a man, and I don't want to jump from that situation into another that's just as hopeless."

Ace leaned forward. "It would only be hopeless if we didn't try."

"Ace, don't try to convince me that you're eager to hear a yes from me. I appreciated your candor last night. You said very clearly that you weren't thrilled, and..."

"Just stop right there!" Blair blinked at him. "Have you given any real thought to the baby?" he questioned.

Instantly defensive, Blair snapped, "More than you have, I'm sure!"

"Are you thinking of him or her as a person? As a human being?"

Blair rolled her eyes. "No, I'm thinking of him or her as a kitten! For crying out loud, I'm the one who's pregnant. What else do you think a pregnant woman thinks about? The baby is constantly on my mind."

He sat back, but his expression was skeptical, speculative. "I can't help feeling that you'd accept my marriage proposal without a qualm if the baby was truly important to you."

"My qualms would fill a bushel basket, Ace, and I'm not apologizing for them, either. It's not like you and I knew each other a long time before we . . . before we . . ."

"Say it. I guarantee it won't kill you," Ace said softly.

Blair brushed a lock of hair back from her forehead. "I don't have to say it. You were there."

"Yeah, I was. I was also there last night."

As dark as it was getting, Blair still saw the sudden hot light in his eyes. Her own eyes dropped to her lap. "What were we talking about? Oh, yes, my vacation. When I get back . . ."

"Where are you going?"

"To a lake cabin."

"A resort?"

"No, it's a private cabin, about a hundred miles from here. When I get back . . ."

"Just a minute. How private are you talking about?"

"Dammit, stop grilling me! It's a very nice cabin on a pretty little fishing lake. That's all I know. I'll be getting the road map tomorrow from Martha Wicks."

Ace ignored that "grilling" retort. "Who's Martha Wicks?"

Blair sighed impatiently. "She works at the Houghton Travel Agency."

"I have a sneaking suspicion that this cabin is off the beaten path," Ace said with a dark scowl of disapproval.

"So?" Blair spoke belligerently.

"So you shouldn't be going out there all by yourself!" Ace got up to pace. "What if something happens?"

"Good grief, nothing is going to happen," Blair groaned. "Honestly, if a stranger overheard this conversation, he'd think you were my father."

"Not *your* father, Blair. Your lover, and the father of your baby."

"At this point, fatherhood gives you absolutely no say in anything I might do," she said sharply. "And let me make myself clear on something. Two occasions—*two mistakes*—do not constitute a relationship."

"In your opinion," Ace retorted. "My opinion says otherwise."

Getting angrier by the second, Blair jumped up. "Just what do you want from me? You're not in love with me, any more than I'm in love with you. Do you actually believe that waltzing off to a preacher is the best conclusion to our situation?"

Ace pushed his face close to hers. "It's the only conclusion that makes any sense. And how do you know I'm not in love with you?"

Blair's breath caught in her throat. "Are you?"

They were nearly toe-to-toe, staring into each other's eyes. "Maybe," Ace finally said.

Blair looked away to conceal the sudden piercing ache in her chest that had to show in her eyes. "Yeah, right. Well, *maybe* I care. Good night. I'm going in. I've got things to do in the house."

Ace caught her by the arm before she could go through the slider. "Blair, wait. I'm sorry. I never say the right thing with you. I always come here hoping for some genuine communication, and we never quite get there. It's probably my fault, because things just aren't very clear in my mind."

He looked miserable, Blair saw. Retreating from anger, she sighed. "It's my fault, too. I know we're not communicating, and I think we're both trying. But that's one of the reasons why we shouldn't rush into anything." Blair paused to dampen her lips. Her voice became gentler. "Sex just isn't enough, Ace."

"I was your first lover, honey, so you couldn't possibly know how special we are together."

"How many lovers have you had, Ace?" she whispered.

His face changed colors. "Don't ask me that."

"A dozen? Twenty?"

"What I did in the past has nothing to do with you." Ace tried to smile. "But it wasn't twenty."

She looked into his blue, blue eyes and thought of all the women he'd taken to bed—not twenty, but a whole lot more than one. A jagged, painful jealousy suddenly ripped at her insides. Other women knew his body, how he kissed, how deep and husky his voice got while making love. It wasn't fair!

"Don't think about it," Ace pleaded raggedly.

"You brought it up," she reminded, her voice unsteady.

"Not in that context."

"No, you were referring to my complete lack of a love life before you, not how many times you . . ."

"Blair, stop it." He gave her arm a shake. "Look, why don't you let me come with you on Saturday?"

Her eyes widened. "On my vacation? Ace, you're the reason I need to get away."

His face darkened again. "That's a damned low blow. You're not going to be able to figure things out by yourself."

"I sure couldn't do it with you there. I need to think, Ace."

"That's the silliest thing I've ever heard," he muttered. "It makes much better sense for the two of us to spend some quality time together."

"Quality time? Like we spent last night?" Blair shook off his hand. "If you came up there, you'd do your ever-loving best to keep me in bed for the entire two weeks!"

He couldn't prevent a grin. "Sounds like a plan to me, sugar."

"But not to me, Ace." Blair stepped through the slider and turned around to close it. "Good night, Ace. I'll let you know when I get back."

Not only was the slider closed in his face, so was the drape. Scowling, Ace traipsed around the side of Blair's house to his truck. Blair made him mad enough to spit nails. What did she expect from him? He'd offered marriage, hadn't he? What else could he do?

Blair left Houghton shortly after eight on Saturday morning. The day was fabulous, full of sunshine and late-summer breezes. Her sense of freedom was only temporary, she knew, but it felt good to drive with the windows down and contemplate two whole weeks without routines or demands. She estimated a two-hour drive to reach the cabin, and most of it would be through familiar country.

Oddly, her marvelous mood began dissipating about halfway through the trip. Instead of the smile she had started out with, she realized that not only had her face become tense, she was gripping the steering wheel much too tightly.

Forcing herself to relax, she switched on the radio. Ten minutes later she deemed it distracting and turned it off. Ace's image seemed embedded in her mind, that and her situation. But those disconcerting apparitions nagged without solutions. Was she wrong to want a real marriage? Was Ace right about her qualms being secondary to the only solution that had any merit, getting married?

She was probably going to do it, Blair thought uneasily. When she got back, she was probably going to call Ace and agree to a farce of a marriage, even though agreeing would be sentencing them both to some extended misery. If only they loved each other out of bed like they did *in* bed! Lord, if that ever happened they would have the best marriage in recorded history!

Reaching the gravel road, Blair drove at a slower speed. Martha's map clearly depicted the route, and indeed, it was taking Blair into an extremely isolated area. But it was also extremely beautiful. She drove through lush pine forests interspersed with open meadows, and recognized a rolling terrain that gradually ascended into the mountains. The air was cooler. The sun filtered through the trees and dappled the road ahead of the car, a pleasing sight.

Finally she saw the cut in the trees Martha had told her to watch for. Blair took the right turn, drove another two miles and suddenly, there was the lake and cabin. The setting was incredible. The cabin was situated on a gently sloping hillside, a pretty structure constructed of highly varnished, peeled logs; the lake was indeed small, but it shone like a mirror and Blair could see about a dozen dark-feathered ducks swimming near the shore; and the views seemed endless, mountains so heavily treed they looked more like a sea of green, peaks of more distant mountains, some of them snow-capped, and sky, lots and lots of blue sky.

Blair's spirit seemed to sigh. This was wonderful, the most peaceful place she'd ever seen. If she couldn't sort through her problems out here, then she couldn't do it anywhere.

By Tuesday afternoon Blair had explored every inch of the cabin, hiked clear around the lake, sunbathed until it became boring, caught two fish with the owner's fishing gear, sat on the cabin's front porch until her haunches ached from immobility, watched the ducks until her head was swimming their same patterns, and read a novel from cover to cover.

Nothing had changed. Her uncertain future was still uncertain; Thorpe Wilson Barclay was still a gunslinger called "Ace,"; and her own emotions were still a swirl of confusion that remained baffling.

One thing she had sorted out, or come close to understanding, at least, was Ace's nebulous connection to Derek. If she hadn't been engaged to Derek when she met Ace, she might not have been so snotty about the accident. In retrospect, Derek's attitude had worried her a lot more than the condition of her car.

Blair's meandering thoughts always brought her back to one searing question. Why was she so responsive to Ace when she never had been with any other man? Her sexuality with Ace felt like a brick wall whenever she sought an answer, an unmovable force that could neither be plowed through nor evaded by detouring around it. If part of her was in love with Ace—her most sensual part—why didn't the rest of her feel the same? For that matter, why was he so plainspoken about wanting her physically and so noncommittal otherwise?

And then, on Tuesday afternoon, again seated on one of the porch's chairs and staring absently at the lake, Blair thought of the baby. Without warning, something strange happened inside of her. It felt like a flower opening, a revelation. *She was going to have a baby!*

A baby was growing and developing in her womb this very minute! Her hands locked together over her lower abdomen. Tears filled her eyes. This was life's biggest miracle. Her mother had felt this same emotion while carrying her and Mitch. "Oh, Mom," Blair whispered, longing for her mother's love and common sense right now.

For the first time since Dr. Miller's verdict, Blair felt as one with her unborn child. Already she loved him or her. Already she could visualize holding the infant, caring for her baby, watching him or her grow, take his first steps, say her first words.

The child is real, she thought while wiping the tears from beneath her eyes. Real and alive and a part of me. Was that what Ace was attempting to convey when he'd talked about the baby being a person, a human being?

Blair sighed. Her and Ace's inability to communicate was a major deterrent to any kind of durable relationship. But had she done any better with Derek? Oh, they had talked more, but then they had spent a lot more time together. And when it finally came down to a serious difference of opinion, they hadn't communicated, either.

Getting up, Blair placed her hands on the porch railing and noticed that the sun was starting its late-afternoon descent. It got dark earlier in the mountains than it did on lower ground, she thought listlessly. If the cabin had a telephone, she might call Ace just to talk a little. Sighing again, admitting some loneliness out here all by herself, Blair left the railing and started into the house to see about supper.

A motor noise brought her up short. "What in the world?" she mumbled, going to the end of the porch from which she could see the road through the trees.

Her jaw dropped when Ace's old pickup drove into the clearing. Talking to him on the phone was one thing, but having him show up was something else. Was she yet ready to deal with his brand of persuasion?

On the other hand, hadn't her choices dribbled down to only one? Her baby deserved the best start possible, and her insisting on illegitimacy when he could have a normal home and both parents wasn't it.

Ace got out. "Hi."

"Hi."

"Surprised to see me?" He started walking toward the porch and Blair.

"Actually, no." Blair managed a small smile as Ace came up the porch steps. "You must have charmed Martha Wicks to get information out of her, right?"

Ace grinned. "Used my best gunslinger smiles, sugar."

"Like you're doing now."

Ace's grin faded. "I hope not." His gaze flicked down Blair's old T-shirt and shorts, then back up to her face. "How've you been doing out here?"

"Just fine. I was just going in to see about supper. Join me?"

"Thanks."

Blair stopped short of the screen door. "Oh, what do you think of the view?"

Ace took a brief look at the lake and mountains. "It's nice, but you're nicer."

Her heart took a dive. "Am I, Ace?"

"Honey, you're the nicest thing to look at I've ever seen," he said in a sensual undertone.

"Did you come up here to flirt?" she whispered.

"Among other things, yes."

Blair swallowed. "Uh . . . let's see about supper."

"Coward," he said softly.

In the kitchen Blair opened the refrigerator. "Supper won't be fancy. I was just going to have a sandwich and a salad."

"Sounds good to me." Ace perched on a stool at the counter. "Let me know if you want some help."

"Thanks, I will." Carrying items from the refrigerator to the counter, Blair asked casually, "Why, really, did you come?"

"To see how you're doing." After a beat he added, "Did you get your thinking done?"

"Yes, as a matter of fact."

"And?"

Blair stopped tearing lettuce and let their gazes meld. "I..."

"Go on, honey. You what?"

Her chin lifted slightly. "Getting married seems best for the baby."

Ace sat perfectly still. "It's best for all of us, Blair."

She didn't look away. "That remains to be seen, Ace."

"What are you afraid of?" he asked softly.

"I'm afraid of a lot of things. Disliking the situation so much we end up disliking each other, for one. I'm afraid of your being unhappy, and of myself being unhappy. I'm afraid that a forced marriage could feel like a trap after a while. And," she added quietly, dropping her gaze to the lettuce in her hands, "I'm afraid of... infidelity."

"Mine, or yours?"

Her eyes flew up. "Not mine!"

"Then you're talking about me." Deserting the stool, Ace came around the counter. "Are you planning to keep me out of your bed after we're married?"

Blair's face flamed. "Of course not!"

"Then why would I turn to another woman?" Blair had averted her eyes, and he took her chin in his hand. "Look at me, Blair."

"I don't like this conversation."

"It's one we have to have. Listen to me, and listen well. I will never—let me repeat that—I will never be unfaithful to you unless you, yourself, force me into it. There's two sides to this coin, Blair. You're a sensual woman. How do I know you won't find another man?"

"Because I wouldn't. I simply wouldn't!"

"Those questions are the same ones that any couple planning marriage has to face, Blair. It's all based on trust."

She swallowed. "Derek...trusted me."

Ace's gaze flicked down to her mouth. Derek had trusted her and she had made love with Ace Barclay. The truth was insidious when examined in this context. "But you weren't in love with Derek, were you?" New and startling ideas were battering both of them. A little bit thunderstruck, they stared at each other. "Trust isn't quite enough, is it?" Ace said huskily. "Nothing is except...love."

Blair took a long breath. "Now you're beginning to grasp what I've been grappling with. Aren't you a little afraid, too?"

Breaking all contact with her, Ace turned away. "I don't know. I'm going to go for a walk. Do you mind?"

"I don't mind," she whispered, deeply shaken by the past few minutes. "I'll let you know when supper's ready."

Eleven

———

It struck Blair while Ace was outside taking his walk that she might have soured him on the idea of marrying her, which hadn't been her intent. But if he came back and announced that he had changed his mind, she had only herself to blame.

Nervously she prepared a green salad and set out bread, cold meat and cheese for sandwiches. You can deal with whatever he decides, she told herself with a sudden fierce determination while placing plates and cutlery on the table. Basically she'd said nothing wrong to Ace. Neither had his comments to her been out of line.

Her nervousness came rushing back, and she froze for a minute. Why on earth had she mentioned Derek? Why remind Ace now that in the most crucial sense of the word she had once been unfaithful? And why hadn't she remembered that herself and stopped her big mouth from practically accusing Ace of infidelity the first time he became disenchanted with their arrangement? Had she lost her mind along with her virtue this summer?

Finally everything was ready in the kitchen. Anxiously Blair teetered through the cabin to the front screen door. Ace was down by the lake, his back to her, his hands in the hind pockets of his jeans. Her vision blurred suddenly. That man out there had offered marriage the second he found out she was pregnant. Even before that, when her condition was merely a suspicion in her own mind. He was the man who lifted her to the stars with his kisses, the man whom she thought to be the most handsome in the world, the sexiest, most magnetic, most appealing, the most ... the most ...

"The best of everything," Blair whispered in dismay. A barrage of burning questions struck without warning. Was she in love with Thorpe Wilson Barclay? In love with Ace Barclay, gunslinger? In love with his body, his charm, his lopsided grin, his flashing blue eyes, his swaggering walk? It was all very possible, wasn't it? Blair's heart sank: she had stupidly put up the most damaging roadblock any woman could ever devise to divert a man's affection.

She wiped her eyes. Crying now was like closing the barn door after the horse had already escaped. Ace had said "maybe" when she'd asked him point-blank about being in love with her, and "maybe" was a demoralizing word. Blair sighed again. Their chance at love seemed weaker by the minute, especially now when she didn't even know if he was going to go through with the marriage.

"Ace," she called. "Supper's on the table."

He turned. "Be right there."

Was his voice different, cooler, his walk less confident? Blair studied every nuance of his form and movements during his hike up the hill to the porch stairs. The shoe had changed feet so abruptly in her case, she felt addled. Why hadn't she seriously wrangled with the implications of her feelings before this?

"The lake is lovely, isn't it?" she said, striving for a note of normalcy in this bewildering situation.

This time he didn't say he would rather look at her. "It's a nice little lake, all right."

Blair held the screen door open. "The bathroom's down the hall if you want to wash up."

"Thanks. I'll only be a minute."

Darting to the kitchen, Blair poured milk into two glasses and set them on the table. Her heart was beating like a tom-tom. "You utter fool," she whispered, meaning it for no one but herself.

Ace walked in. "Did I just hear you talking to yourself?"

Blair shaped a shaky smile. "Been alone too long, I guess. Sit down. Everything's ready."

They made sandwiches and heaped their plates with salad. Blair kept shooting Ace uneasy glances. Was he avoiding direct contact with her eyes? Was he searching his mind for a way to let her down easily? *Babe, you've been right all along about forced marriages. It would never work.*

"Are you still planning to stay here for two weeks?" Ace asked.

Blair took a swallow of milk. "I'm a little undecided now."

"Because of our plans?"

Blair's eyes widened. Maybe he *was* still planning to marry her!

"Yes, because of our plans," she said evenly, though her heart had gone wild in her chest.

"We probably should get married right away," Ace said. "While you've got some time off." He leaned forward slightly. "Do you intend to keep on working?"

The question startled her. "Yes, of course."

"What about after the baby comes?"

"I . . . haven't thought that far ahead."

"But we'll live at the ranch."

Blair was pushing lettuce and tomatoes around on her plate with her fork. "That's what I've been thinking, yes." She raised her eyes. "Is that what you want?"

"I couldn't live in town. What will you do with your house?"

"My brother and I will have to work that out. Mitch is half owner."

"Speaking of your brother...do you want him at the wedding?"

Blair sat back to admit rather dejectedly, "That's something else I haven't considered." It was true. She hadn't weighed her job *or* Mitch's participation in the wedding. All of her determination to "think things through" had been focused on Ace.

Now she knew why. All along deeper and more important feelings for Ace than she'd consciously acknowledged had been festering. When had she fallen for him, before they had made love? During? Afterward?

She wanted to ask him again if there was the slightest possibility of him having similar thoughts about her. *Is there any chance at all that you might be in love with me?* Yet, looking at him across the table and remembering his evasive answer to that question before, all she could do was wish for the courage to freely speak her mind.

Neither of them ate with any show of hunger or genuine enjoyment. Blair realized that they were at the table merely because it was the time of day for a meal. Any previous spontaneity between them had disappeared, and it was her doing, her fault. Ace was going to go through with the marriage because to him it was the right thing to do, and if he *had* felt something important for her at one time, her endless procrastination, her doubts, and her demeaning attitude had destroyed it.

Sighing silently, she pushed her plate back. Ace set an unfinished sandwich on his. Their gazes met and locked across the table.

"So," he finally said quietly. "What comes next?"

"Next?"

"Yes, next. When do we do it?"

"Get married, you mean?" Her voice sounded hollow. "I don't know. Maybe Mitch should be there. He should be told about it, at least. He might be hurt if I just did it without...telling him ahead." Her weak voice trailed off. There had to be a way to repair the damage she'd inflicted earlier with those inane comments and questions about fidelity. Ace's eyes looked empty, and she'd never seen his expressions as empty before. As reserved, she amended. His reserve now was frightening. What if he never teased her again? Or called her "sugar," or looked at her as if she were a delicious morsel?

She had never been generous with Ace. Maybe that was what was needed now. "I'd like you to stay the night," she said, speaking quietly.

His pupils seemed to contract as he regarded her with an unwavering gaze. "Any particular reason?"

"Would you stay if I didn't give you a reason? Or if I put off giving you my reason until—" Blair took an unsteady breath "—maybe in the morning?"

Ace leaned back in his chair with a thoughtful expression. Understanding Blair wasn't getting any easier. If anything, she was becoming more complex. But she hadn't issued this sort of invitation before, and he was curious about what she had in mind.

Besides, he hadn't arrived here intending to drive right back to Houghton. An overnight case containing his shaving gear and a change of clothes was in his pickup. Still, their almost farcical relationship had taken another disturbing twist, and grasping its implications was still eluding him.

"You didn't want me here at all, and now you want me to stay overnight," he said softly. "How should I interpret that?"

"At face value."

"In other words, just do it without questioning it."

"I know it's asking a lot, but..." Blair braved a direct meeting with his eyes. "It could be important."

This was her ball game, Ace thought then. Whatever it was that Blair was cooking up, was he in any position to refuse? And maybe it was important. Maybe a night together was what they needed.

"All right," he said abruptly. "I'll leave it all in your hands. I'll stay. Anything else is up to you."

Blair's eyes narrowed slightly. It was up to her? She had hoped an invitation to stay the night would activate his imagination. "Um... fine," she said uneasily. Her own imagination had them in her bedroom, the obvious place in which to explore her feelings, and his. But how would she get him there without a bluntly stated "Ace, come to bed with me."

No, that was out. She was female, wasn't she? A romantic being? Blair sighed to herself. She used to think of herself as romantic; now she just didn't know. Deliberately setting out to seduce a man was beyond her realm of experience.

Still, could it be that difficult? A few props, a little perfume, some seductive words? Surely she could manage.

She got to her feet. "Would you mind taking another walk?"

Ace rose, slowly. "How long do you want me to be out of the cabin?" This could prove to be a very interesting night.

She had no idea how long it would take her to bathe and set the scene. "Um... why don't I turn on the porch light when I want you to come back? Would that work for you?"

Ace glanced to the window. Twilight was setting in. "The porch light would work fine." Indolently his gaze traveled down Blair's T-shirt and shorts. He would bet anything that when he came back she would be wearing something else, maybe a sexy nightie. "The porch light's a good idea. I'll watch for it."

That look bolstered Blair's courage. Ace might have some compunctions about their relationship, but he was still an extremely sexual man. And he knew she had intimacy in mind, how could he not? Would he really leave it all up to her? If she went to him right this second and put her arms around him, wouldn't he take over and whisk her into the bedroom?

Looking into his eyes, she realized they were no longer empty. In fact, she was positive that she saw a spark of amusement. Or was it devilry? Could he be enjoying this?

Maybe she was enjoying it, too. Certainly a pleasurable tension was building within her. Her lips twitched with the hint of a smile. "Don't go too far. I shouldn't be long."

"See you later," he said casually, and avoiding even a brushing contact as he passed her, he left the room.

Blair sucked in a suddenly necessary breath. The opening and closing of the front screen door reached her ears, Ace's boots on the porch and stairs, and then silence. He was gone, out of the cabin.

She sprang into action, clearing the table, dropping the dishes into the sink, forgetting them at once and rushing down the hall to the bedroom she was using. Her wardrobe was limited, *very* limited. What would she put on? Frantically she checked her few clothes in the closet. Everything she'd brought along was for a solitary, sexless vacation!

But she had to do something special! Darting into the bathroom, she turned on the faucets for the tub. At least she had some bath salts in her favorite scent with her, and she threw in a handful.

Now what? Her mind raced. Candles! There was a whole drawer of candles in the kitchen. Racing through the cabin, Blair filled a large bowl with the candles, took a stack of saucers from the cabinet, found some matches and brought the whole shebang to the bedroom. It took at least five minutes to melt wax in each saucer to hold the candles upright. Rushing to the bathroom to turn off the water flowing into the tub, she returned to the bedroom to spend another five minutes deciding where to place so many candles.

Finally she undressed and jumped into the tub of hot, scented water.

Outside, Ace stood at the water's edge. Every few minutes he glanced back at the cabin to check the porch light. Wondering what Blair was doing to prepare for the night was causing his blood to heat up.

But aside from a physical excitement he didn't even attempt to allay, his thoughts were serious. He'd never dwelled much on the idea of marriage, and he would soon be a married man. Blair would be his wife. They were going to have a baby. He had *better* be serious about so much change, he figured in a moment of wryness.

That revelation about nothing other than love having the power to make a marriage work had hit him hard. Blair was important to him, but how did a man know when he was in love with one particular woman? Did an almost-constant craving for her body constitute love? If that was the case, he was madly in love with his wife-to-be. He'd always functioned normally with attractive women, but Blair had him ditzy with lust most of the time. Maybe that was love. Certainly lust had to be a major component.

And yet she had thought herself in love with Derek, obviously without lust. Strange.

Thinking of Blair with Derek—though he still hadn't set eyes on the man—delivered a powerful blow to Ace's system. She'd been on the verge of marrying Derek Kingston and would have followed through without Ace's intervention. If she and Derek hadn't spent their time making love, what *had* they done together?

Stars were beginning to appear in the darkening sky. Ace lifted his eyes to scan the pinpoints of brightness. The night air was cool, bordering on chilly. Fall was just around the corner; winter wouldn't be far behind. His child would be born in April.

Maybe by April he and Blair would have learned to do together whatever it was that she and Derek had done. Right now they needed no lessons in bed, but out of bed they didn't do so well.

Glancing at the cabin, Ace's heart lurched in his chest. The porch light was on.

Blair heard him coming, his footsteps on the porch, the opening of the screen door, then a moment of silence, probably when he realized how dark the interior of the house was. "Blair?" She stayed silent. A light came on in the cabin's main room and went out again. She held her breath.

Ace blinked in the dark, but the few seconds of light had given him his bearings. He headed for the same hall in which he'd located the bathroom earlier. Another door was ajar with about a two-inch crack of dim light. He flicked the door open and felt his heart sliding down . . . down.

The room was lit by candles, dozens of them, perched on the dressers, on a table, on the windowsill, on the bed stand. In the middle of the bed was Blair. Something creamy—a sheet, maybe—was wrapped around her like a sarong. Her hair gleamed. Her lips were glossy and slightly parted in a little half smile that he saw as mysterious.

"Nice," he said huskily. "Very nice."

"Come in." He took two steps into the room. "I wanted music," she said softly. "But I couldn't get anything but static on the radio. Is there a storm brewing outside?"

"None that I noticed."

"I thought maybe there was some sort of electrical disturbance," she murmured.

"I think there is, but it's not going on outside."

She arched an eyebrow. "Meaning it's in here?"

"What do you think?"

She smiled. "I think you should stop standing there and come over here."

Ace gestured at the candles. "I thought you liked the dark."

Blair languidly adjusted her position, stretching out a leg. "Not tonight."

Moving unhurriedly, he approached the bed. "You make a mighty pretty picture lying there. You're an exciting woman, sugar."

Uh, oh, Blair thought. If he was resorting to cocky endearments, then he wasn't a hundred percent sure of himself.

Or maybe, in this case, he wasn't sure of her. Given their rocky history, it wouldn't be at all unnatural for him to be wondering why she had suddenly turned seductive.

It wasn't a topic she wished to discuss right now. "You're an exciting man, Ace," she said instead, speaking in a low and sultry voice. The husky timbre of her voice wasn't pretense. Her senses were reeling, from the setting she had devised herself, from the hot light she could see in Ace's eyes.

"Am I?" He sat on the edge of the bed. The air was redolent with perfume, a fragrance he had come to associate with Blair, though normally she used it sparingly, subtly. His right hand rose to the buttons on his shirt.

"Let me." Sitting up, Blair scooted closer. Ace dropped his hand and let her undo his buttons. His blood was racing. His gaze flicked over Blair's face while she slid buttons through buttonholes. Her eyes darted to his then down again.

He dampened his lips. "I like you this way."

Her fingers stopped moving. "I'd hoped you would." Their eyes met.

He stifled the word *why*. Yet the questions remained in his mind. *Why did you go to so much trouble tonight? Why the candles and perfume? Why have you put me off time and again, even to telling me that I was the reason you needed to get away by yourself, and then do this after I came without an invitation?*

Something had driven Ace to come out here, even without Blair's blessing. Since the last time he'd seen her, an inner voice had nagged and pestered him. Admittedly he didn't like her being alone so far from town, but it wasn't her safety that had gnawed at him, it was her. His mouth tightened. Maybe he *was* in love with her. Would she laugh if he said so? Flip the idea away as preposterous?

The reality of their relationship wasn't comforting. They were great in bed and getting married out of necessity. She, apparently, was enough of a realist to accept their sexuality and let it go at that. Shouldn't he do the same?

Fine, he thought with a sudden surge of anger. He would cooperate fully tonight. Only, he wasn't going to make it easy for Blair. Why should he? She knew he wanted her every time they were together; it was time to uncover what *she* wanted.

He sat there, concealing his jagged and discomfiting thoughts, while her fingers flitted from button to button. She slid his shirt open and pressed her lips to his chest. His heart began thumping loudly. "Sometimes I think the word *mysterious* was created to describe women," he whispered hoarsely.

She laughed softly, deep in her throat. "Are you saying you don't understand me, Ace?"

"How could I? One minute you're as cool as ice and the next you're a siren."

"A siren and a gunslinger," she whispered between kisses to his chest. "We're quite a pair, wouldn't you say?"

His jaw was clenched, his eyes closed. "You still think I'm just a guy on the make, don't you?"

"No."

He opened his eyes to tip her chin. "Then why do you call me that?"

Blair studied the dark depths of his eyes. "I think I like the term. To me it describes a handsome, sexy man who knows how to make a woman feel like a woman. You can't deny you fit that description, Ace."

He grinned slightly. "I should sit here and agree to thinking of myself as handsome and sexy? Wouldn't that be a little egocentric?"

"Which you are." Blair raised her hand and lightly caressed his lips. "Which you should be," she added in a near whisper. "You are handsome and sexy, Ace. And I'm never more womanly than when I'm in your arms."

Every trace of levity vanished from Ace's face. "That works two ways, Blair. You make me soar."

A strong gust of wind hit the cabin, and the candles flickered. "Make me soar, Ace," Blair whispered. "You're the only man who's ever been able to do it."

Their desire for each other was suddenly all that mattered. Ace wound his fingers into her tangled curls and lowered his head. His kiss to her lips created the final spark, and groaning, they fell back on the bed. In seconds Blair's makeshift sarong had become merely a sheet again, and lay in a puddle beneath her.

Her skin was rosy in the candlelight, flushed from inner heat and Ace's caresses. "You are so beautiful," he whispered raggedly. As he kissed her hungrily, his hand skimmed down her belly to the moist curls between her thighs. Hungry, too, Blair tugged at his belt buckle. She felt him kicking off his boots.

He broke away for a moment to shed his clothes, and she raised up to an elbow to watch, her expression rapt and adoring. This has to be love, she thought dreamily. Love in its most elemental form. Certainly she loved his body, his physicality, his power over her senses.

Nude, he gathered her into his arms, and the connection of bare skin to bare skin was like an electrical shock. But it was a shock of pleasure, not of discomfort, and they sought more of the same, snuggling closer and moving against each other.

There was no longer a question of morality in Blair's mind. However sudden and unexpected their first encounter, she now belonged—at least bodily—to Thorpe Wilson Barclay, and she felt at home in his arms. She sighed with the thought and prayed for a truly united future.

His ultimate possession was so welcome, Blair felt tears in her eyes. "Ace . . . oh, Ace," she whispered.

He raised up to see her face, and her tears deeply touched him. For a moment words of affection rose in his throat. He nearly said them. "Blair . . ." Something stopped the uninhibited flow. If he gave everything . . . But what *was* everything? Was he sure enough of his feelings to be spouting off about them?

A great tenderness began controlling his hands, his lips, his body. Though he couldn't say what was in his heart, he was driven to lavish Blair with warmth, with emotion. She responded in kind, and their lovemaking took on a quality that had them both in awe.

In the end it was as wild and wonderful as before. Blair swore she touched the stars, and Ace was so replete he wondered if he would ever feel sexually aroused again. They lay there in the candlelight, unmoving for the longest time, utterly satisfied, totally at peace.

Finally they stirred. Ace slid over on the bed and tucked her into the circle of his arms. Contentedly Blair sighed. He whispered into her hair, "Did you soar, sweetheart?"

She smiled serenely. "I soared . . . and I soared . . . and I soared."

He laughed softly. "Good." His eyes closed.

But Blair's eyes were suddenly wide open. Now they should talk. How should she begin the conversation? *Ace, I'd like to talk about love.* No, that was too abrupt. *Ace, have you ever been in love?* But then she might hear about another woman. *Ace, wouldn't you prefer a more complete marriage over what we have planned so far?* Too inane. Of course he would prefer the whole ball of wax. Who wouldn't?

She frowned. Instigating a discussion about love wasn't a simple matter. She could blurt it out, of course. *Ace, I'm in love with you. Or . . . I think I am. No, I'm almost positive. Consider me in love with you. Can you do that? Can you think of me and love in the same thought?*

But what if he looked at her as though she had suddenly slipped a cog. Would she ever get over the hurt?

Maybe it was best to let nature take its course. Wouldn't his feelings—if he had any that were truly serious—come out eventually without any prodding from her?

There *were* feelings between them, she thought then with heartfelt passion. There were. It was just that they had started out so badly, with him tossing gunslinger endearments and grins around and her refusing his every advance.

Until that evening in his bedroom when things had gotten so out of hand, she reminded herself with a long sigh. But then there'd been Derek to consider, and her own life-long morality to deal with. She had shocked herself into some sort of emotional immobility, and it had taken her quite a while to come out of it.

That was where she was now, wasn't it? Thinking more clearly again, able to weigh her feelings and give them the value they deserved?

But Ace was still mired in that same stage of indecision in which she'd been floundering until today. He had tried very hard to get past her objections to anything between them during the first days of their acquaintanceship, and maybe he was afraid of trying again. Or maybe he was tired of being turned down.

And yet, here they were in the same bed, wrapped around each other, sated from lovemaking that had been much more than mere sexual gratification.

Maybe, in their case, *sex* was enough.

Maybe it was all they would ever have.

Twelve

At some point before sleeping, Blair slipped from Ace's arms and extinguished the candles. The next morning she realized that she had done so on automatic pilot because the incident was very fuzzy in her mind. A second event in the night also seemed wrapped in layers of cotton candy, making slow, delicious love in the dark under warm blankets.

She awoke to bright sunlight, feeling mellow and ecstatically happy. She and Ace had reached a new plateau, even if they hadn't declared undying love for each other. Gradually they were becoming close. Eventually the time would be right to talk about feelings.

Turning over in bed, Blair was disappointed to find herself alone. Obviously Ace had awakened before her, but where was he? The cabin was silent, so maybe he was outside.

Bounding out of bed, Blair grabbed her robe and headed for the bathroom and a shower. She hummed while she bathed and thought eagerly of the day ahead. Surely Ace wouldn't rush off this morning. The isolation of the cabin and lake was wonderful for lovers. They could make love on the tiny beach, should they choose.

Blair laughed joyously at the notion. Before meeting Ace she never would have envisioned making love in the great outdoors. For that matter, making love at all had seldom entered her mind. Because of Ace, she had become a sensual woman.

Because of Ace, she had become a *happy* woman.

Well, she still possessed a few pockets of unease, she had to admit. But everything was moving along so well between them now, and she was sure it would only get better.

Dressed and ready for the day, Blair went to look for Ace. The cabin was vacant, so she went to the front door and peered out. As she had thought, he was down by the lake.

She stepped out onto the porch. "Hey, handsome! Want some breakfast?"

Ace turned and grinned. "Finally got up, huh?"

"How long have you been up?"

"An hour or so." Ace began trudging up the hill. "You were sleeping and I tried not to wake you."

Blair descended the stairs to meet him and just naturally stepped into his arms. They kissed, once, twice, a third time, each mating of their mouths warmer than its predecessor. Blair looked into his eyes and murmured, "Maybe you'd prefer having your breakfast in bed."

He brought her hips forward, letting her know that idea was entirely possible. "It's a thought, sweetheart."

She touched his lips with her fingertips. "Let me ask you this. Are you planning to leave in the very near future?"

"Anxious for me to go?"

"I'd much rather you stayed, but . . . if you have to get back to the ranch . . ."

He kissed her fingers. "There's no hurry. Virge is there. I can stay until late this afternoon, at least."

"I'm glad."

"Are you, Blair?" Ace was as sober as Blair had ever seen him.

"Yes," she said simply, and considered this another step forward for them. Her smile flashed. "Now, food or..." She let the inference dangle.

Ace laughed. "My stomach's growling. Guess it had better be food."

Arm in arm they climbed the porch stairs and went into the cabin. "What would you like, eggs or cereal?" Blair asked as they headed for the kitchen. "I know. How about some French toast?"

"Sounds great."

Blair did most of the cooking. Ace's assistance was more hindrance than help, but they shared a kiss every few minutes and there was lots of touching. Blair's happiness expanded.

What happened after the French toast had been consumed made her happier still. They talked. Sitting at the table over numerous cups of coffee for Ace and herbal tea for Blair, she told him about her parents, her brother and growing up in Houghton, and he detailed his life in Colorado. "Would you like your brother and his family to attend our wedding?" she interjected at one point.

Ace sat back and thought about it. "Dave just might come," he said after a moment. "I should let him know."

Blair nodded. "I agree."

"I'll call him this evening. But let's decide on a date so I have something concrete to tell him."

Blair became very still. "Does this coming weekend suit you?"

"It suits me just fine. Does it suit you?"

Their gazes locked across the table. They were discussing their wedding date with no more passion than if they were making a date to see a movie.

"Yes," she said quietly. To dispel the pall she felt overpowering her previous enthusiasm, she stood up. "How about a hike around the lake?"

Ace got to his feet. "Should you be doing that?"

"I've already done it once. Walking is something the doctor recommended I do every day. Besides, I'm bursting with energy." She smiled. "Come on. I'll do the dishes later. It's a gorgeous day. Let's not let all that sunshine go to waste."

"Okay," he agreed. Blair knew better than he what she should or should not do during her pregnancy, and a hike around the little lake was an appealing pastime.

Outside, they cut to the right of the lake. "There isn't really a path," Blair explained. "But there are only a few spots where the way isn't clear. I didn't have any trouble at all with the terrain."

About a quarter of the way around, they stopped to watch a flock of ducks on the water. "I did some fishing the other day," Blair said. "And I caught two nice trout."

"You like to fish?"

"Don't sound so surprised," Blair said teasingly. "I enjoy fishing. Why are you laughing?"

"That is something I couldn't have guessed in a million years, babe."

"There just might be a lot of things about me you could never guess, Ace Barclay." Flipping her hair back pertly, she strolled away. "Give that some thought."

Grinning, he watched the sassy swaying of her hips as she went. "What you're making me think about with that sexy sashay just might cut this hike short," he called.

Giggling under her breath, Blair kept going. Ace caught up with her and took her hand. On the far side of the lake they stopped again and looked across the water to the cabin. "It's really very pretty, isn't it?" Blair murmured.

"Who owns it?"

"I haven't met him. Martha said he's very cautious about who he rents to."

"I don't blame him, it's a nice place. Apparently you passed muster."

Blair smiled. "I have a good reputation, Mr. Barclay."

"Is that why you're marrying me, to maintain your good reputation?"

Blair hesitated, then said slowly, "We talked about that before, Ace, without reaching any definite conclusions. I've thought about it, naturally, and maybe you should tell me if it would bother you if my decision had been influenced by a dread of gossip.''

He took and then released a long breath. ''Guess it would only be normal.''

''Yes, but . . .'' She closed her mouth. He hadn't told her what she'd wanted to know at all, but forcing a more definitive reply from him didn't seem prudent. They were both getting used to their new status. Until last night they'd been little more than antagonists, though their conflict most certainly had never consisted of clear-cut and precisely separated viewpoints. Today they were different with each other, much closer, and Blair wasn't going to undermine their progress with probing analyses of everything he said and did.

Quieter than they'd been, each involved in their own thoughts, they began walking again. After a few minutes Blair exclaimed, ''Oh, look! There's a trail through the trees. I didn't notice it when I was out here before. Let's find out where it goes.''

''Blair . . .''

''Come on. Don't be a spoilsport.'' Blair took off on the narrow trail.

Without knowing why, Ace wasn't thrilled with the detour. Following the configuration of the lake had been easy going; exploring completely unknown ground felt wrong for some reason. Ordinarily, new territory just begged him to investigate, but the strangest premonition in this instance had him feeling as tight as a drum.

''Blair, let's turn back.'' The trees and brush were so tightly packed they looked woven together. ''Come on. This is far enough.''

''There's a clearing ahead,'' she called over her shoulder. ''I want to see what's there.''

Frowning, he kept walking. But his footsteps lagged, and Blair was at least fifteen feet ahead. And then, without warning, she disappeared.

"Blair!" he yelled a bit grouchily, his first thought being that she was playing hide-and-seek with him. His second thought was one of concern; she had truly vanished! Running at full speed, he almost went over the embankment himself, barely managing to stop in time. Blair was at the bottom of a ten-foot drop, lying still and silent. "Blair!" Ace began scrambling down the steep bank, his heart in his throat.

He knelt beside her. "Blair...my God...Blair..." He touched her face. Her eyes were closed, her skin pale. Then he saw the rock under her head. "Oh, God," he moaned. "Blair...wake up." Lightly he slapped her cheek. "Honey...Blair..." He checked her pulse, relieved to find it erratic but strong.

She was unconscious. This was a dangerous spot. There should have been a warning sign. Fury fogged his vision, but he cast it away and tried to think. She'd hit her head, but had she also sustained other injuries? How would he know? He couldn't just leave her here alone and go for help.

Swiftly he scanned the embankment. Some distance away it sloped to an easy climb. Carefully he slid his forearms under Blair's limp body, maneuvered himself into a rising position and heaved himself to his feet. He began walking, his mind racing.

The cabin didn't have a phone. He remembered how surprised he'd been when Martha Wicks told him it had everything but a phone. "It's the owner's preference, Ace," Martha had explained. "Blair understood the isolation completely when she rented the place."

Blair understanding this god-awful isolation was small consolation for Ace. Superhuman strength had him carrying Blair as though she were an infant. His strides were long and purposeful. He refused to think the worst. He would get her back to town and to a doctor, and she would be fine.

But the trek went on and on. He went back the way they had come as that direction was familiar to him. He kept looking for signs of consciousness from Blair, but she never moved. His arms began aching. His breathing became labored.

But he never slowed down, and finally the cabin was within reach, and his pickup. Uncertainty arose. Was it best to put her to bed and go for help? He weighed the matter during the final torturous steps, and ultimately decided that he couldn't leave her here alone.

Yet she should be lying down for the long drive. Her car! Yes, it made better sense to take her car. The muscles in his arms were trembling, but he managed to open the back door of her sedan and then to cautiously arrange Blair on the seat. He paused to catch his breath and realized there was blood on his shirtsleeve from the gash on her head. Terror gripped him, suddenly, fiercely, and it took a minute to beat down the panic.

Loping to the cabin, he raced to the bedroom and began searching for Blair's car keys. He found a purse in a dresser drawer and rifled the bag until he located a key ring. Grabbing a pillow and blanket off the bed, he ran back outside, gently slid the pillow under Blair's head and covered her with the blanket.

Grimly he got behind the wheel, started the car and took off.

There were sounds...vague...far away. Gradually they became louder, more defined. Muffled footsteps... voices...someone crying. Who was sobbing like that?

Blair's eyelids lifted a fraction. The light hurt her eyes and she closed them again. Her head hurt. What had happened? Where was she?

That crying. Who was weeping so grievously? Her eyes blinked open. A dark head was bent, broad shoulders were shaking... Ace! She was in a bed, and he was hunched over it from a chair. And he was crying.

She lifted a hand, a monumental effort, and laid it on his hair. "Oh, my dear," she whispered. "What could possibly be that bad?"

His head jerked up. His face was sodden with tears. "You're awake." Wiping his face, he got up and hurried away.

"Ace?" Bewildered, she allowed her eyelids to droop and shut out the light.

"Blair? Open your eyes."

She obeyed the authoritative voice and saw a strange face peering down at her. She licked her dry lips. "Where am I?"

"In the hospital. I'm Dr. Ingram. Can you see me clearly?"

"I think so, yes."

A sharp, probing light was shone into her eyes. "You received quite a blow to the head, young woman. You have a slight concussion." After a few minutes of examination, the doctor added, "You're going to be fine. Just don't be in a hurry to get out of bed. I want you here for tonight and possibly tomorrow. We'll see how you're doing then."

He turned to Ace and spoke quietly. "I'll leave the rest to you."

Ace nodded silently. His eyes were red and he didn't care who saw them, either. None of the other sorrows of his life had prepared him for this one, and he was dealing with it on a minute-by-minute basis.

Blair was gingerly touching the bandage on her head. With the doctor's exit, Ace sat on the edge of the bed. "How're you feeling?"

"Awful. My head is pounding."

"They're cautious about giving pain medication to people with head injuries." He took Blair's hand and held it.

"What happened out there?" she whispered.

"You don't remember falling?"

She frowned. "Vaguely."

"It happened so suddenly. There's a ten-foot drop in the trail, and there isn't anything out there indicating the danger."

"How did I get to the hospital?"

"I brought you."

"You must have carried me out of there."

"Yes."

She studied Ace's red eyes. "Why were you crying?"

He swallowed. "There's no kind way to tell you this, Blair. You—" his voice broke "—lost the baby."

At first it didn't register. "But I only hit my head. Why would..." Her body stiffened. "Oh, no! Ace, you must be mistaken. Who told you that? How? Why?" She began weeping.

"Easy, honey." His voice was thick and unsteady. "I don't have any answers—neither do the doctors—but you have to be strong."

She didn't want to be strong. She wanted to burrow into her misery. The pain in her head was minor compared to the pain in her soul. Her baby was dead. Why? Her mother had always maintained that whenever God closed a door, he always left a window open. She struggled to find that window, and there were only cold, blank walls.

Tears were spilling from Ace's eyes again. Bending over Blair, he held her. Words came without design. "Take it easy, honey. Everything will be all right. You'll have other babies."

Nothing he said or did soothed Blair's pain. The baby had been created by accident...and had died by another accident. She felt submerged in agony, pummeled by guilt. It was her fault. She should have listened to Ace and not run blithely down that unfamiliar trail.

Next came self-pity. What had she ever done to deserve so much pain? Her sobs increased.

"Blair...don't, honey. Try to calm down," Ace pleaded. Sitting up, he dried his own tears.

Thinking of the child again, she turned her face away and covered it with both hands. "I can't bear it...I can't," she sobbed. "It's my fault. I killed our baby."

Ace grabbed her hands and pulled them away from her face. "Listen to me. It was an accident."

"It's my fault!" she practically screamed. Ace's stricken face registered, but the sight of his sorrow only made her feel terribly weary. "Please go away. I'd like to be alone."

"I don't want to leave you like this."

"Go. Please." Her voice turned bitter. "You don't have to marry me now. I'm no longer your responsibility. Please just leave me alone."

Her rejection felt like a knife in Ace's heart. "You're hurting right now," he said hoarsely. "And you're only lashing out at me to—"

"You're wrong. Yes, I'm hurting, but what I said is the truth. You did the honorable thing, so your conscience is clear. What I'm feeling is between me and my baby." She burst into tears again. "Go away!"

He hadn't expected this from Blair. In truth, he hadn't attempted to analyze how she might react to the tragedy, but he never could have imagined her turning on him like this. As torn up as he was himself, he couldn't help resenting her harsh, accusing attitude.

Sliding from the bed, he stood up. "I'll come back later."

She didn't answer, merely turned her head on the pillow to avoid looking at him, and received a blinding jolt in her head for her effort. Wincing, she closed her eyes.

Ace stood there and looked at her broodingly for a minute, then spun on his heel and walked out.

Blair listlessly picked at the dinner delivered to her bed. Her headache had diminished to a tolerable ache because of the pain pills she had finally been permitted after another visit from Dr. Ingram. A second doctor, a gynecologist, had come in to discuss the miscarriage.

"There was no damage to your organs, Blair, so you will be able to have other children. Losing a baby affects different women in different ways, so your deep sorrow is not unnatural. There is one thing I would like to say, which may or may not give you some comfort. Nature sometimes has its own way of dealing with an imperfect fetus. You may have miscarried even without that fall."

"You're saying my baby wasn't perfect?"

"I'm saying that it's a possibility. Try not to blame yourself."

The doctor's message was clear but not entirely acceptable to Blair. She had fallen unnecessarily, and it was difficult to relegate her own negligence to a mere step in nature's grand scheme.

Martha Wicks had also stopped by that afternoon. "This is awful, Blair, but you must understand that you had wandered away from the property you rented."

"I don't intend to sue anyone," Blair said dully. "If that's what you're worried about."

"It did cross my mind," Martha admitted. "The owner feels terrible about your mishap, but he really bears no responsibility."

"Tell him to relax. I accept full responsibility."

Those words haunted Blair while she pushed peas around on her dinner plate. Martha hadn't known about the miscarriage and Blair hadn't explained. Other than a few doctors and nurses, Ace and herself, no one would ever know. That small life had sparked and died with very little recognition, and it was so terribly sad.

But she hadn't been very nice to Ace, and he had been devastated. Never had she heard a man weep so brokenheartedly, and it was stunning to realize just how hard he'd been hit by the miscarriage. Had he loved their baby more than she'd known? More than he'd indicated?

A woman came in for the dinner tray. "You didn't eat a whole lot, young lady."

"Maybe tomorrow," Blair murmured. Alone again, she sighed heavily and stared out the window at the fading sunlight. This morning she'd been so happy, and this evening she felt like the stale dregs at the bottom of a day-old cup of coffee. She should probably be grateful that her head injury wasn't more serious than it was, but gratitude for her own well-being was difficult to assemble when everything had changed so drastically.

It had been a summer of changes, she thought as if viewing the season from afar. A summer of emotional highs and lows. She had come close to marrying two men. Derek had been a mistake in judgment and Ace was . . .

Blair bit her lip to hold back a sob. Ace was now and always would be the most important man in her life. She wouldn't always be sad, as she was now. Things would get back on track. She had her job, and her brother, and eventually she would return to normal.

But years from now, no matter what else had happened, no matter whom she had met or what she had done, Ace would still be the most important person she had ever known.

"Hi."

Blair turned her face to the door. Ace was standing there with a bouquet of flowers. Her heart seemed to turn over in her chest. "Hi," she whispered.

He came in. "I brought you some flowers."

She found her voice. "They're beautiful. Thank you. Are they in a vase?"

"Sure are. Where should I put them?"

"Over there on that table where I can see them."

He deposited the vase and came to stand by the bed. "Feeling any better?"

"Much better. Dr. Ingram prescribed some pain pills this afternoon. They helped a lot." Her eyes met his. "Sit down, if you like."

"Thanks." Ace moved a chair over to the bed and sat down. "Did you have dinner?"

"About fifteen minutes ago." He looked haggard, Blair realized. A little gray, a little pinched around the mouth. "Are you all right?"

"Don't worry about me. I'm fine."

"You weren't fine before."

"Yeah, well, I'm fine now."

Blair fell silent. If he didn't want to talk about his earlier distress, she could hardly force him to do so. But wasn't it sad that he couldn't admit his sorrow, that they couldn't commiserate together?

He spoke abruptly. "There's something I want to say."

"Go ahead," she said, willing to listen to anything he might have to say. What did they have now? Was there any hope at all for the two of them?

Ace's eyes rose to study the ceiling. "I thought about it all day. I think I knew it before today, but it never quite gelled, if you know what I mean. Anyway, it's this." Ace brought his gaze down to level on her face. "I love you. I wish I'd said it before, but there it is. I . . . love you."

Stunned, Blair stared for the longest time. He stared back. "Say something," he finally urged.

She took a breath. "The only thing I can think of to say is that I love you, too."

They stared again. "You do? Are you sure?"

"I've been sure since yesterday. That's why I asked you to stay overnight. I'd hoped . . . we might reach the point of talking about our feelings." Blair's voice had no strength. Her body had no strength. Never could she have imagined this scene. Especially not after today's frightful events.

"But we never did. Even while making love we didn't *mention* love." Ace's mouth twisted with some bitterness. "It took a tragedy to make me understand what was in my own damned soul. Blair, when I saw you lying there, my fear was for you. During the drive to town I started worrying about the baby. The emergency room people took over then, and all I could do was pray. I should have stopped you on that trail. I *knew* it wasn't safe."

Blair lifted her hand. "Come closer." Ace transferred himself from the chair to the bed. "Dearest," she said softly, emotionally. "You told me not to blame myself. You must follow your own advice. Neither of us could have anticipated what happened, and we both have to stop looking for someone to blame." She saw the tears in his eyes and felt the sting of her own.

He put his arms around her and they wept together, clinging to each other, finally united in their grief.

"We'll have other babies," Ace whispered raggedly. "I love you so much, Blair."

"Yes, my love." Her reassurance was for Ace, as she couldn't bear his unhappiness. In her heart would always remain one immutable ache for the tiny life that had touched hers so briefly. There were some things a woman never forgot.

But Ace wouldn't forget, either, and neither of them had to spell it out. They knew, both of them, and their eyes and caresses contained a newly gained tenderness because of today.

They wiped away their tears with tissues and tried to smile at each other. "We'll wait until you're completely well, but then we'll get married," Ace said quietly.

"And we'll invite our families to the wedding."

"We'll invite everyone."

"Ace?"

"What, honey?"

"Call me *sugar*."

His expression reflected surprise. "Right now?"

"Right now."

Some of his old cockiness flashed in a grin. "Do you still think I'm a gunslinger?"

"By all means. But you're *my* gunslinger, Ace Barclay, and I will love you for the rest of my days."

"I love you, too, sugar. Forever and always."

Blair settled back with a soft smile for her beloved. "Everything's going to be all right," she murmured.

And . . . she knew it was true.

Epilogue

Blair stopped short, her astonished gaze locked on a gaudy tent and sign.

"Anything wrong?" Ace laid his arm around his wife's shoulder and peered into her face. "Are you all right?"

Blair stood frozen. This couldn't be the same carnival that had been in Montana last summer, could it? She and Ace were in California on their honeymoon. They had been married exactly five days, most of which had been spent in a luxury suite at the Pacific King Resort. Today they had rented a car and taken in some of the coastal sights. Ace had spotted the carnival and laughingly insisted they stop. After merrily walking through the crowds, taking a few of the rides and gorging on hot dogs and popcorn, they were headed back to their car.

"Blair?"

She could hear the concern in Ace's voice. There were moments when one of them would lapse into a melancholy silence. Blair knew that was what had Ace worried now. Neither of them wanted his or her spouse unhappy, and when it happened, the other always hastened to break the somber mood.

But that tent...that sign. She couldn't ignore this startling coincidence. "I'm fine, darling," she murmured. "But I think I'd like to have my fortune told by Madam Morova. Would you mind?"

Relieved that nothing was amiss, Ace chuckled. "You don't really believe in that stuff, do you?"

"I'm not sure. Would you wait out here for me? It won't take long."

Ace smiled indulgently. "Sure, go ahead. I'll get a cup of coffee at that stand over there."

Blair tore her attention from the tent to give her husband a kiss on the cheek. "Thanks." She saw his smile, his sky blue eyes, his wonderful mouth, and for a moment the crowds and noise vanished. "I love you."

He caught her around the waist for a passionate, if brief, embrace. "I love you, too. Forever and always."

"Forever and always," she whispered.

Then she walked away, skirting groups of people, and approached the ticket booth outside the tent. "One, please," she murmured, passing money through the window.

"You can go right in," the ticket seller told her.

"Thank you."

Gingerly, with a quickened heartbeat and a decision to pay closer attention to detail than she had before, Blair went to the tent's entrance. The hanging fabrics were familiar to her memory of her first encounter with Madam Morova, and as before, the cacophony of exterior sounds all but disappeared when she stepped inside the enclosure. Though there was little light, Blair was aware of colors—mauve, plum, deep blue, pearlescent gray. There was a scent in the air, not cloyingly sweet or heavy as she might have expected, but something pleasant and relaxing.

"Please sit at the table."

Blair turned toward the voice and watched Madam Morova materialize from the shadows. Her makeup was just as pronounced as Blair remembered, and if anything, there were even more gold chains around the woman's neck than before.

Nodding slightly, Blair seated herself. Madam Morova took the other chair and laid her hands on the table, palms up. "Place your hands in mine."

Blair noted the woman's long painted fingernails and false eyelashes while laying her hands in hers. Common sense told her that Madam Morova had to be a fake, a woman who was clever enough to fabricate intriguing tales to accompany the clues she picked up from her clients' own person. Today, for instance, she was bound to recognize the rings on Blair's left hand as a wedding set, and few people could misinterpret the glow in Blair's eyes. Almost anyone would be able to conclude that she was newly married.

And yet, how had the fortune-teller accurately predicted Blair meeting and marrying Ace?

"We have met before," Madam Morova said softly.

Disconcerted, Blair blinked. "Um . . . yes."

"You have undergone a recent sadness." Blair swallowed hard and started to speak. "Please say nothing." The woman closed her eyes. Wide-eyed, Blair stared at her across the table. "Despite the sadness, you are at peace. There is excitement in your life, and much happiness. You have traveled recently, and you will travel again very soon."

After a silent moment the woman opened her eyes and said in a strangely perplexed voice, "Because I see nothing unusual in your future, I will allow you to ask a question. Is there anything you would like to know?"

Blair sat there. The woman's hands were warm and smooth. The fragrance and muted atmosphere of the tent were tranquilizing. She knew that her earlier doubts had evolved into an uneasy belief. Madam Morova's simple statements concerning travel and Blair's present state of mind, and her more complex comment regarding a recent sadness had dissolved the doubts Blair had brought into this tent. Besides, the woman *had* accurately predicted meeting and marrying Ace, right down to their autumn wedding.

Yet the only question Blair wished an answer for was so close to her heart she was afraid to risk asking it. A negative response might cause her irreparable damage, and she didn't want to leave this tent and return to Ace with a forlorn face.

"You are thinking of a certain topic," Madame Morova observed quietly. "One that brings a note of tragedy to your lovely eyes. It is related to a recent experience, is it not?"

"Yes," Blair whispered. "I . . . I had a miscarriage."

"Ah, I see the problem. You wish to know if there will be other children." Again the fortune-teller's heavily mascaraed lashes dropped to cover her eyes.

Blair waited expectantly, sliding forward to sit on the edge of her chair. She shouldn't be here, and certainly she never should have allowed this question to arise. A doctor was the logical person with whom to initiate this topic, not a carnival fortune-teller.

And yet she allowed Madam Morova to concentrate, to ruminate. A second later the woman began speaking. . . .

Leaning against the metal-pipe fencing encircling the Ferris wheel, Ace watched the crowd while sipping coffee from a foam cup. Colorado and Montana had their share of odd ducks, but nothing like California did, he thought with good humor and an inward grin. One guy walking past had purple-and-magenta hair. Three young girls sauntered by giggling over a private joke, which was perfectly normal. Only, one girl's head was shaved bald, another's was shaved around her ears, and the third girl had hair that had been bleached in stripes and hung down to her hips. There were ordinary people, too, of course. Lots of families. Lots of kids. Ace stifled a sigh.

"Hi, handsome."

Ace turned to see Blair standing beside him. "Hi, beautiful." He grinned. "Did you learn all the secrets of the future?"

"Before I answer that, let me tell you about something that happened several months ago." Taking Ace's arm, Blair started them walking toward the parking lot. "This same carnival was in Missoula last summer, although I didn't recognize it until I saw Madam Morova's tent and sign. Anyway, I had the woman tell my fortune at that time, and..."

"The same woman?"

"The same. Isn't that eerie? I mean, here we are in California, and we only planned this trip about two weeks ago."

"Eerie," Ace repeated in a tongue-in-cheek manner and with a teasing twinkle in his eyes.

"I know you're not impressed, and I know you don't believe in things like fortune-telling, but maybe you'll be a little less skeptical when you hear what she told me in Missoula."

They had reached their rental car. Ace unlocked the passenger door and Blair got in while he ambled around the front of the vehicle and climbed in the driver's side. As the car was stuffy, they rolled down the windows. Ace turned in the seat. "Tell me what she said in Missoula."

"Promise not to laugh."

He nodded solemnly. "You have my word."

Blair took a breath. "Well...we had never set eyes on each other before that day, you have to remember. I walked into her tent and she told me to sit at the table. She laid her hands on the table like this." Blair turned her hands so her palms were up. "Then she said, 'Place your hands in mine.' I did it, and I knew she could feel my engagement ring, even though she wasn't looking at it."

"Derek's ring," Ace said quietly.

Blair looked into his eyes. "Derek was right outside the tent, Ace. In fact, he was the one who insisted I have my fortune told."

"Why'd he do that?"

"Just for fun, I'm sure. Please don't be upset because I mentioned Derek."

"I'm not at all upset, honey. Go on with your story."

Blair squeezed her husband's hand. "Well, I knew she was aware of my ring, so when she started talking about a wedding in my future, I became quite smug about her transparency. Only, she wasn't talking about my and Derek's wedding. She said I would marry a dark, handsome man, and that I would have a fall wedding. I got a little huffy and told her my fiancé was blond and that we were having a summer wedding.

"Then, Ace, she said, 'You haven't yet met the man you will marry.'"

Ace sat there without moving. "When did you say this happened?"

"About a week before I met you."

After a moment Ace gave a brief, somewhat startled laugh. "It's coincidence, Blair, it has to be."

"Do you really think the woman's prediction was nothing but a lucky guess? Doesn't it make you feel just a little bit odd? It does me. I thought about it after I got home the day you ran into my car. I had just met a dark, handsome stranger."

Ace's outlaw grin flashed. "Did you really think I was handsome that first day?"

"I thought you were the most devastatingly handsome... the most *dangerously* handsome rat I had ever met."

"Rat, huh?"

"Or snake. Take your pick," Blair said while smiling sweetly.

Ace caught the back of his wife's head and pulled her forward for a deep and sexy kiss. At the same time his hand slithered under her skirt. Blair whispered against his lips, "Don't forget where we are, lover."

Raising his head, Ace looked out at the parking lot and groaned. "Maybe it's time we returned to the Pacific King Resort and that king-size bed."

"Obviously," Blair murmured.

Ace let go of her and started the car. Maneuvering through the parking lot, he tossed Blair a glance. "So it's your opinion the woman is genuinely psychic?"

"I'm almost afraid to speculate on that. Until this experience I'd never believed in the occult, but everything she told me that day came true."

"What did she tell you today?"

A giggle welled in Blair's throat. "It might be better if I kept that to myself."

"Don't leave me hanging now, honey. What did she say?"

"That we're going to have seven children," Blair said in a very meek voice.

"*What?*" At his stunned and stricken expression, Blair's laughter erupted. "Blair, I'm not sure that's funny."

"I think you're beginning to believe," Blair gasped between spasms of giggles.

"She said seven? Are you sure?"

"There's absolutely no similarity in the pronunciation of seven and two, or seven and one, Ace. She said seven. I'm sure of it."

Driving into the parking lot of the Pacific King Resort, Ace found a space near the door closest to their unit and stopped the car. He looked at his bride. "Seven kids. Blair... are you pulling my leg?"

She lovingly touched his face. "Let's go in, darling. I wouldn't dream of pulling your leg in public, but in private there's no telling what I might do."

He trapped her hand in his. "First tell me the truth. Did that woman really tell you we're going to have seven kids?"

"That's exactly what she said," Blair said softly.

"Do you believe it?"

Blair smiled. "Do you?"

"The idea makes you happy, doesn't it?"

"It lifts me to the stars, Ace."

"You're so beautiful you make my teeth hurt," he whispered gruffly. "If you want seven kids, then we'll have seven kids. Let's go inside and get started on number one."

Blair cleared her throat. "On numbers one, two and three. If we are to believe Madam Morova's prediction, our first three are going to be triplets." Ace paled before her very eyes. "Darling, right now I don't care how many children we have as long as we're blessed with one. And Madam Morova is, after all, only a carnival fortune-teller."

They stared into each other's eyes. "You're right," Ace said gruffly, hoarsely. "She is only a carnival fortune-teller. Let's keep our heads straight and try to remember that."

Blair smiled serenely. "I couldn't agree more, my love. We never have to mention it again."

* * * * *

Get Ready to be Swept Away by
Silhouette's Spring Collection

Abduction
& Seduction

These passion-filled stories explore both the dangerous
desires of men and the seductive powers of women.
Written by three of our most celebrated authors, they are
sure to capture your hearts.

Diana Palmer
Brings us a spin-off of her Long, Tall Texans series

Joan Johnston
Crafts a beguiling Western romance

Rebecca Brandewyne
New York Times bestselling author
makes a smashing contemporary debut

Available in March at your favorite retail outlet.

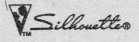

MILLION DOLLAR SWEEPSTAKES (III)

SILHOUETTE®
Desire
Hearts of Stone

Three strong-willed Texas siblings whose rock-hard protective walls are about to come tumblin' down!

A new Silhouette Desire miniseries by

BARBARA McCAULEY

March 1995

TEXAS HEAT (Silhouette Desire #917)
Rugged rancher Jake Stone had just found out that he had a long-lost half sister—and he was determined to get to know her. Problem was, her legal guardian and aunt, sultry Savannah Roberts, was intent on keeping him at arm's length.

August 1995

TEXAS TEMPTATION (Silhouette Desire #948)
Jared Stone had lived with a desperate guilt. Now he had a shot to make everything right again—until the one woman he couldn't have became the only woman he wanted.

Winter 1995

TEXAS PRIDE
Raised with a couple of overprotective brothers, Jessica Stone *hated* to be told what to do. So when her sexy new foreman started trying to run her life, Jessica's pride said she had to put a stop to it. But her heart said something *entirely* different....